"The twists and turns in the novel leave the reader frantically turning the pages. This book is a perfect read for anyone who appreciates classic cinema, a good mystery, and a love story set in Paris."

—*Fresh Fiction*

PRAISE FOR *THE INGREDIENTS OF LOVE*

"A frothy *exposé* of the perils of book packaging, seasoned with a soupcon of culinary courtship . . . Lovers of Paris and voyeurs of the French publishing scene will find much to relish."

—*Kirkus Reviews*

"These are *The Ingredients of Love*: a delightful heroine, a mysterious hero, romance, Paris, and beaucoup de charme!"

—**Ellen Sussman, *New York Times* bestselling author of *French Lessons***

LOVE
LETTERS
from
MONTMARTRE

Also by Nicolas Barreau

The Ingredients of Love
One Evening in Paris
The Secret Paris Cinema Club
Paris is Always a Good Idea

LOVE LETTERS

from

MONTMARTRE

A Novel

NICOLAS BARREAU
TRANSLATED BY RACHEL HILDEBRANDT

Arcade Publishing • New York
A Herman Graf book

Copyright © 2019 by Nicolas Barreau

First published in the United Kingdom by Piatkus, an imprint of Little, Brown Book Group.

First US Edition 2020

Arcade Publishing books may be purchased in bulk at special discounts for sales promotion, corporate gifts, fund-raising, or educational purposes. Special editions can also be created to specifications. For details, contact the Special Sales Department, Arcade Publishing, 307 West 36th Street, 11th Floor, New York, NY 10018 or arcade@ skyhorsepublishing.com.

Arcade Publishing® is a registered trademark of Skyhorse Publishing, Inc.®, a Delaware corporation.

Visit our website at www.arcadepub.com.

10 9 8 7 6 5 4 3 2 1

Library of Congress Cataloging-in-Publication Data is available on file.
Library of Congress Control Number: 2020932856

Cover design by Erin Seaward-Hiatt
Cover photo credit © Zefart/Getty Images (Montmartre image); © Tetiana Lazunova/Getty Images (postmark)

Print ISBN: 978-1-950691-52-4
Ebook ISBN: 978-1-950691-58-6

Printed in the United States of America

*To my mother who first showed me the grave of
Heinrich Heine at the beautiful cemetery of Montmartre*

Come, my love,
be mine again
like once in May

LOVE
LETTERS
from
MONTMARTRE

Prologue

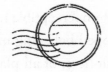

Montmartre – that famous hill on the northern edge of Paris, where tourists cluster around the street painters on the Place du Tertre as they create artworks of dubious quality, where couples ramble hand in hand through the lively springtime streets before sinking down a little breathless on the steps of the Sacré-Cœur, to gaze in amazement across the city shimmering in the final gentle rosy glow before nightfall – Montmartre is home to a cemetery. It is a very old cemetery, complete with dirt paths and long shady drives that meander under lindens and maples. It even uses names and numbers, which make it seem like a real town – a very silent town. Some of the people resting here are famous. You can find graves ornamented with artistic monuments and angelic figures in flowing stone garments, their arms gracefully outstretched, eyes fixed on the sky.

A dark-haired man enters the cemetery, holding the hand of a young boy. He stops at a grave known only to a few people. No one famous slumbers here. No author, musician or painter. This isn't the Lady of the Camellias, either. Just someone who had been deeply loved.

Nonetheless, the angel on the bronze tablet attached to the marble gravestone is one of the loveliest here. The woman's face – earnest, perhaps even serene – gazes out, her long hair billowing around her face as if being tossed by a wind at her back. The man stands there while the child scampers around the graves, stalking colourful wings.

'Look, Papa. A beautiful butterfly!' he cries. 'Isn't it wonderful?'

The man gives an almost imperceptible nod. Nothing is beautiful to him any more, and he stopped believing in wonders long ago. There is no way he can know that here, of all places, something wonderful is going to happen, something that will actually come close to being a wonder. At this point, he feels like the unhappiest person on earth.

He had met his wife in this same Cimetière Montmartre, five years ago at Heinrich Heine's grave. It had been a sun-drenched day in May, as well as the start of something that had been irretrievable for some months now.

The man casts one last look at the bronze angel with the familiar features. He is writing secret letters, but he is unprepared for what will happen, just as unprepared as anyone can be for the arrival of happiness or love. And yet both of them are always there. As a writer, he actually should know that.

The man's name is Julien Azoulay.

And I happen to be Julien Azoulay.

1

The world without you

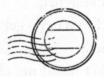

I had just sat down at my desk to fulfil my promise and to finally, finally, write to Hélène, when the doorbell rang. I decided to ignore it, and instead unscrewed my fountain pen and straightened my piece of white paper.

'Dear Hélène.' I stared rather helplessly at the two words that stood there just as lost as I had been feeling for the past year.

How do you write to a person you love more than everything, but who no longer exists? I had suspected back then that I was crazy to make this promise, but Hélène had insisted, and like every other time my wife got something into her head, it was hard to argue against it. She always came out on top in the end. Hélène was very strong-willed. The only thing she'd been unable to defeat was death itself. Its will had

3

been stronger than hers.

The doorbell chimed again, but I was already far away. I smiled bitterly and could still see her pale face and green eyes, which seemed to widen above her sunken cheeks with each passing day.

'After I die, I want you to write me thirty-three letters,' she had said, her eyes boring deep into mine. 'One letter for each year of my life. Promise me this, Julien.'

'But what good will it do?' I replied. 'It won't bring you back.'

At that point, I was out of my mind with fear and anguish. I sat day and night beside Hélène's bed, clinging to her hand, unwilling or unable to imagine a life without her.

'Why write letters when I won't ever get an answer? What would be the point?' I continued quietly.

She acted as if she hadn't heard my objection. 'Just write to me. Describe what the world is like without me. Write about yourself and Arthur.' She smiled as tears gathered in my eyes.

'It will have a point, trust me. I'm sure that when all's said and done, there'll be an answer for you. And wherever I happen to be, I'll read your letters and be watching out for both of you.'

I shook my head and started to weep.

'I can't do it, Hélène. I just can't!'

I didn't mean the thirty-three letters, but rather just everything. My entire life without her. Without Hélène.

She watched me with a gentle gaze, and the pity that shone from her eyes broke my heart.

'My poor darling,' she said, and I could feel how much effort it took for her to squeeze my hand encouragingly. 'You have to be strong now, so you can take care of Arthur. He needs you so much.'

And then she said what she had said so many times over the past few weeks since that devastating diagnosis. Unlike me, this admission seemed to give her the strength to face the end with serenity.

'We all have to die, Julien. It's completely normal and part of life itself. I've just reached this point a little earlier than expected. I'm not happy about it, believe me, but it's just the way it is.' She gave a helpless shrug. 'Come here and kiss me.'

I brushed a coppery curl back from her forehead and pressed my lips gently against hers. She had grown so fragile over these final months of a life cut far too short. Every time I gingerly hugged her, I was scared I might break something, even though pretty much everything was already destroyed. Only her courage stayed intact, and it was much stronger than my own.

'Promise,' she ordered once more, and I caught a little glint in her eyes. 'I bet that by the time you've written the last letter, your life will have taken a turn for the better.'

'I'm afraid you'll lose this bet.'

'I promise you I won't.' A knowing smile flickered across her face, and her eyelids fluttered. 'And when that happens, I want a giant bouquet of roses from you – the biggest in the whole damned Cimetière Montmartre.'

That was Hélène. Even in the lowest of moments, she managed to make you smile. I cried and laughed at the same time, as she held out her frail hand. I shook it and gave her my word.

The word of an author. In any case, she never specified when I should write those letters to her. So October turned into November, which then slipped into December. One sad month followed another. The seasons might change their plumage, but for me, everything

5

remained the same. The sun had plummeted from the sky, and I lived in a pitch-black hole devoid of words. In the meantime, we had reached March, and I still hadn't written any letters. Not a single one.

It wasn't that I hadn't tried. I wanted to keep my promise. It was Hélène's last wish, after all. My waste basket was overflowing with crumpled pages sprinkled with sentences I couldn't seem to end. Sentences like:

My most beloved Hélène, since you've been gone, there's been no . . .

Darling, I'm so weary of all the pain. I find myself asking more and more if life is even . . .

Dearest, yesterday I found the little snow globe from Venice. It was stuck far back in your nightstand, and I couldn't help thinking about how the two of us . . .

Dearest person in the whole world, I miss you every day, every hour, every minute. Do you have any idea . . .

Dear Hélène, yesterday Arthur declared that he doesn't like having such a sad Papa and that you're having fun with the angels . . .

Hélène, mayday, mayday! This is an SOS from a drowning man. Come back, I can't . . .

My angel, I dreamed about you last night and was bewildered when you weren't next to me when I woke up this morning . . .

My greatly missed darling, please don't assume that I've forgotten my promise, but I . . .

I had simply been unable to set onto paper anything more than this helpless stammering. I would just sit there, overwhelmed by despair, and feel the words slip away from me. I hadn't written anything – not exactly a good thing for a writer to admit – and that was also the reason there was now a storm brewing outside.

With a sigh, I set my pen back down on the desk, stood up and walked over to the window. Down on Rue Jacob stood a small, elegantly dressed gentleman in a navy-blue raincoat. It was obvious he had no intention of removing his finger from my doorbell any time soon, and my fears had come true.

The man glanced up into the damp spring sky, at the clouds skittering in front of the driving wind. I jerked my head back.

It was Jean-Pierre Favre, my publisher.

Ever since I can remember, I have moved through a world of beautiful words. I started out working as a journalist, then as a screenplay author. I eventually wrote my first novel, a romantic comedy that struck a nerve and surprised us all by becoming a bestseller. People always say that Paris is the City of Love, but that doesn't necessarily apply to what interests Parisian publishers. Back then, I received one rejection after another, when I received any response at all. But then one day a small press contacted me, one located on the Rue de Seine. While his fellow publishers focused on literary and intellectual fiction, Jean-Pierre Favre, the publisher at Éditions Garamond, was fascinated with my amusing little romance packed with all sorts of tragicomedic entanglements.

'I'm sixty-three years old, and not much can make me laugh at this point,' he explained during our first meeting at Café de Flore. 'Monsieur Azoulay, your book made me laugh, and that's more than can be said about most books these days. As you get older, you laugh less and less anyway, believe me.' With a deep sigh, he sank back into the leather bench in front of the window on the second floor where we had found a quiet table. He raised his hands in mock despair. 'I often wonder where the authors who can write really good comedies have gone? Something with heart and wit. But no! They all want to write about hopelessness, decay, grand drama – drama, drama, drama.' He struck his palm against his forehead, where his grey hair had begun to thin, the strands combed elegantly back. 'Urban depression, murderous nannies, visions of horror, terrorism . . .' He brushed a few breadcrumbs from the table. 'Everything has its place, but . . .' He bent forward and gazed hard at me with his pale eyes. 'I want to tell you something, young man. A good comedy is much harder to write than people think. The ability to conjure up something wonderfully light but without platitudes, something that leaves us with the feeling that life is worth living despite everything – that is true art! I, at least, am too old for stories where after reading them you think you'd best locate the nearest skyscraper to jump out of.' He ripped open three packets of sugar before shaking them into his freshly squeezed orange juice and creating a small whirlpool with his spoon. Then he switched mental gears.

'Or films! Don't get me started on those!'

He paused for effect, and I waited eagerly for what would come next. This man was a brilliant conversationalist, that much I already knew.

'Nothing except tristesse and ambitious convolutions. Everyone today wants to be one thing in particular: unique. But I want to laugh, does that make sense? I want something that will make my heart pound.' He grabbed a handful of the sky-blue waistcoat he was wearing underneath his suit jacket and took a large gulp from his juice glass. A youthful grin stole across his face.

'Did you see that film about the Japanese butcher who falls in love with his pig? The one that ends with them committing double suicide through hara-kiri? I mean, who comes up with stuff like that?' He shook his head. 'People have lost their minds. I really miss the filmmakers like Billy Wilder and Peter Bogdanovich. Their heads were screwed on right.' He tsk-tsked in confirmation of this. 'Trust me, Monsieur Azoulay, life isn't one big walk in the park, which is why we need more books like yours.' He brought his fiery speech to an end and held out his Montblanc fountain pen for me to sign the contract. 'I believe in you.'

That had been six years ago. My novel became a bestseller, and Garamond offered me a three-book deal, which gave me financial security for the next few years and granted me the luxurious freedom of writing full-time. I met auburn-haired Hélène, who loved the poetry of Heinrich Heine and sang Sacha Distel songs in the shower. She became a teacher, got pregnant, and married me. We became the parents of a little boy who, Hélène always insisted, was lucky to have inherited my dark blond hair and not her fiery tresses.

Life was as bright as a summer's day, and everything we put our hands to seemed to meet with success. Until misfortune struck.

'Blood at the wrong time,' Hélène said one morning as she emerged from the bathroom. 'Don't worry, it won't be anything bad.'

But it was bad. Worse than bad. I was the author of romantic comedies that sold amazingly well. That was how I made my livelihood.

And then all of a sudden, my vocabulary was punctuated with deeply troubling words like *colorectal cancer, tumour markers, cisplatin, metastasis, morphine pump, hospice.*

I learned first-hand the truth that life is no walk in the park, despite Hélène's brave face and the first, optimistic, prognosis. After one year, it looked as if the illness had been beaten. It was summer, and we took Arthur on a trip to the Brittany coast. Life was more precious than ever – a gift. We had once again dodged the bullet.

But then Hélène complained about pain in her back.

'I'm slowly turning into an old woman,' she teased as she knotted her vivid pareo around her.

But the cancer had already spread everywhere, clinging like tiny crabs to her body and refusing to be evicted. It was all over by mid-October. The metastases kept on spreading and Hélène was failing along with them. My ever-optimistic, joyful Hélène, who loved to laugh. All the dreams we'd had died with her.

I remained behind, with our little son, a heavy heart, a promise still unkept, and a bank account that was gradually dwindling. It was March, and I hadn't written even one line in over a year. My new novel consisted of fifty pages, and now my publisher was standing at my door, wanting to know how the book was coming.

The ringing stopped.

Monsieur Favre was a real gentleman. He had been extremely sympathetic, and hadn't pressed me over the past year. He had given me time to pull myself together, to recover, to sort myself out, as people like to say. He hadn't mentioned the novel even once, despite having originally planned for it to be released this year, before silently postponing it to next spring.

He had tried to make contact for the first time two weeks ago. The grace period was obviously over. Tentative questions left on my answering machine, which stayed plugged in day and night. A sympathetic letter that concluded with a question. His number appearing over and over again on my cellphone.

I was pretending to be dead, and in a way I was. My creativity had been extinguished. My wit had turned to cynicism. I floundered through my days and was at a permanent loss for words. What could I have said, anyway? That I would never again put anything readable down on paper? That I no longer had words left inside me – a sad, sad man who was supposed to create light-hearted comedies? The irony of fate. God was a sadistic joker, and I was hopelessly lost.

'Drama, drama, drama,' I murmured with a bitter smile as I peered out of the window again.

Monsieur Favre had vanished, and I breathed more easily. He had obviously given up.

I lit a cigarette and glanced at the clock. Three hours to go until I had to pick up Arthur from nursery school. Arthur was the only reason I was still among the living. Why I still got up in the mornings, got dressed, went to the grocer's to buy food. Talked.

My little boy never gave up. He got that from his mother. He would lace his small fingers into mine and drag me over to admire what he had built from Lego. He crawled into bed with me at night and snuggled up against me, trustingly. He drew me into conversations, asked thousands of questions, and made plans. He said things like: 'I want to go to the zoo to see the giraffes,' or: 'Papa, you're scratchy,' or: 'You promised to read to me,' or: 'Is Maman lighter than air now?'

I stubbed out the cigarette and sat back down at the desk. I smoked too much, drank too much. I was subsisting on stomach tablets. I shook another cigarette out of a packet that featured a picture of a smoker's lung. Oh, come on! That's how I was going to end up, but before that point, I would finish at least this one letter – the first of thirty-three, which seemed as superfluous to me as a goitre. Letters to a dead person. I ran my fingers through my hair.

'Oh, Hélène, why, why?' I whispered, staring at the framed picture that sat on the dark green leather desk pad.

It made me jump when the apartment doorbell chimed. Startled, I tugged at the small chain on the old-fashioned green banker's lamp, cutting off the light that had been burning needlessly since early morning. Who could that be? A moment later, someone started pounding on the door.

'Azoulay? Azoulay, open up. I know you're in there!'

Yes, I was in here, in the prison of my own choosing up here on the fourth floor. I couldn't help thinking back a few years, to the time when Hélène and I had met with the real-estate agent in the empty rooms of this old apartment, which we could actually afford with my first royalty payment. The agent had called it a dream apartment: sunny, only a few steps from Boulevard Saint-Germain, but still quiet. But no elevator, Hélène had protested. When we're old, we'll be huffing and puffing by the time we clamber all the way up here. We'd laughed – 'When we're old' had sounded so distant then. How strange, what people think about – and then something completely different comes along.

In any case, Jean-Pierre Favre had successfully entered the apartment building, and had nimbly conquered the stairs as well.

He had probably rung the neighbour's doorbell. Hopefully it hadn't been Cathérine Balland, who had a key to our apartment – in case of emergency.

Cathérine had been my wife's best friend. She lived on her own with her cat Zazie, one floor below us, and had tried to support me as much as she could. Up until five days before Hélène's death, she had kept the faith that everything might still turn out all right. She occasionally babysat Arthur and spent hours playing Uno with him, a card game whose appeal I had never understood. She really was amazingly nice, but she missed Hélène too much to actually provide much consolation. Quite the opposite – I sometimes couldn't bear her 'Oh, Julien . . .' and the mournfully expressive gaze from her half-moon, Julie Delpy eyes.

So far, I hadn't started bawling in front of her. Thank goodness for that.

'Azoulay? Azoulay, don't be silly. I just saw you at the window. Open the door! It's me, Jean-Pierre Favre. Your publisher, remember me? Don't leave me standing out here like an idiot. I just want to talk. Open up!' Renewed pounding.

I stayed in my chair, not moving a single muscle. How could a little man with such perfectly manicured hands muster up so much endurance and strength?

'You can't stay holed up in there for ever,' he bellowed through the door.

Sure I can, I thought defiantly.

I tiptoed over to the hall door, hoping to hear his footsteps fade away down the wooden staircase. But I didn't hear anything. Maybe we were both standing there – me on the inside, he on the outside – holding our breath and straining to listen.

And then there was a noise, the sound of someone tearing a page out of a notebook. Seconds later a white sheet of paper slid under the door.

Azoulay? Are you all right? Please tell me, at least, that everything is fine. You don't have to let me in, but I won't leave until you have given me some sign of life. I'm worried about you.

He clearly assumed I was standing on a chair with a rope around my neck, like the sad hero in *Bread & Tulips*, one of his favourite films. I smiled against my will and softly padded back to my desk.

Everything is fine.

I printed neatly on the page before pushing it back under the door.

Why won't you let me in?

I thought for a moment.

I can't.

This received an immediate response.

What does that mean? Are you naked? Or drunk? Do you have a lady visitor?

I covered my mouth, pressed my lips together, and shook my head. Lady visitor – only Favre would still use such an old-fashioned phrase.

No, no lady visitor. I'm writing.

I shoved the sheet back under the door and waited.

I'm so happy to hear that, Azoulay. It's good that you're writing again. It will help distract you, you'll see. I won't bother you any more. Write, my friend! Let me hear from you. Talk to you soon!

Yes. Soon! I'll be in touch.

I wrote back.

Jean-Pierre Favre hesitated a moment, irresolute, but I then heard his footsteps on the stairs. I hurried to the window and watched him leave the house, his coat collar turned up. With quick little steps, he headed along Rue Jacob towards Boulevard Saint-Germain.

I sat back down at the desk and started to write.

Dear Hélène,

You'd have enjoyed the funeral. That makes it sound as if it were yesterday, and for me it is, although six months have passed since then. Time has stood still since that glittering golden October day that was so unsuited for a funeral and so suited for you, who were always aglow. I hope you can see that I'm finally writing to you. The first of thirty-three pointless letters. No, forgive me. I don't want to be cynical. You wanted this, and we shook on it. I will keep this last promise. You had something in mind, I'm sure of that, even if I have no idea what it might have been.

Everything has become pointless since you left.

But I'm trying, truly I am. You told me that you would read my letters from wherever you happened to be. I really want to believe that my words will somehow reach you.

It's almost spring, Hélène. But spring without you isn't really

15

*spring. The clouds are moving through in clusters. It rains, and
then the sun comes back out again. This year we won't be able
to go for walks through the Jardin du Luxembourg, holding
Arthur's hands and swinging him through the air with a 'one-
two-three upsy-daisy'.*

*I'm afraid I'm not very good at being a single dad. Arthur
complains a lot that I never laugh. Tonight we watched an old
Disney film together, Robin Hood. You know, the one with the
foxes. We've seen it five times this month. When we reached the
scene where Robin Hood and his men use a rope and pulleys to steal
the sacks of gold from bad old Prince John, while he's snoring away
in his bed, Arthur suddenly announced: 'Papa, you have to laugh.
That was really funny!' I tried to smile and pretend like it was.*

*Oh, Hélène! I spend all my time pretending. I pretend to watch
TV, pretend to read, pretend to write, to talk on the phone, to go
shopping, to go for walks, to listen. I pretend to live.*

*Life is so damned hard. I'm trying, you must believe me.
I'm trying to be strong the way you said, to keep on living
without you.*

*But without you, the world is so lonely, Hélène. Without you
I'm lost. It feels like I can't get anything right any more. Anyway,
you would have liked the ceremony. Everyone said it was a
really nice funeral. I know that's a contradiction in itself, but
still . . . I planned everything the way you wanted. I can at least
be proud of that.*

*I found a wonderful spot in the Cimetière Montmartre, right
next to an old chestnut tree. Heinrich Heine's grave isn't too
far away, either. You'd be pleased. I told everyone who came to*

the funeral to wear anything but black, just as you'd asked. On
that October morning – only a few days after your thirty-third
birthday – everything would have been perfect, had we not been
saying goodbye to you for ever. The sun shone, and the leaves
glowed in shades of yellow and red. Everything was peaceful,
almost cheerful. A long procession of brightly dressed guests
trailed behind your coffin with all of its flowers, almost like they
were going to a party of some kind. I wondered if something so
dressy could also be so sad. And yes, it could.

Everyone came. Your father, your brother, and your aunts
and cousins from Burgundy. My mother and her sister Carole,
who even brought along old Paul, her perpetually bewildered
husband, who kept asking every few minutes: 'Who died?'
He forgot again as soon as you told him. All our friends were
there. Even your childhood friend Annie from Honfleur came,
dashing into the cemetery after the ceremony in the chapel had
already ended and we were gathered around the grave. She was
so late because some poor guy had thrown himself in front of her
train. She managed to find a taxi driver willing to drive her at
breakneck speed over the last stretch to Paris. Her arrangement
of roses and lilies was in tatters, but she made it, loyal soul.

So many of your worker friends were there, as well as the students
from your class. The principal said words in the chapel, and the priest
also handled his part with some feeling. The school choir sang the
Ave Maria. I surprised myself by finding it moving. Cathérine gave
a wonderful eulogy, which touched everyone. She was very calm and
collected, and I really admired that. Later she confessed that she'd
taken a sedative. I couldn't manage anything – I'm sure that comes as

no surprise – but I did set up a large photo of you in the chapel – the one of you standing in the giant lavender field, your arms folded as you laugh so exuberantly into the camera. Our first trip together to Provence, remember? You look so happy. It's one of my favourites, even if you always complain that the sun makes you squint.

I picked out a song for you, and it was played as we stood around the grave. 'Tu est le soleil de ma vie', our French version of Stevie Wonder's hit. Because that's what you always were for me, my love, the sunshine of my life.

I couldn't console Arthur when they lowered the coffin into the ground. He clung to me, and then to Mamie. It was horrible for all of us to have to watch you disappear, for ever and irretrievably, into that deep hole. Alexandre stood beside me, like a boulder in the surf, and squeezed my arm.

'Trust me, this is the worst moment,' he said. 'It won't get worse than this.'

This reminded me of the words from Philippe Claudel, who once wrote that eventually we all end up following coffins.

I stood there, frozen, and saw all the flowers and wreaths with the final wishes. I watched my sobbing child who no longer had a mother, and that was the last thing I saw, as the tears wouldn't stop. Things eased up once we reached the restaurant afterward. The guests chattered busily, loaded up their plates, even laughed. Everyone was relieved to be on the other side, and this brought a temporary intimacy and joviality. I even ended up chatting with various people, and eating some of the appetisers because I was suddenly ravenous. Arthur flitted from one person to another, explaining that you had taken all of your suitcases and moved to *heaven, where you would be pretty once more. And that you were bound to be happy to see your Maman again. (I wasn't quite sure about that, though, knowing how difficult your mother was. I just hope you won't end up arguing up there in heaven, where they say great peace and quiet is supposed to reign.)*

Anyway, Arthur imagines that you've been able to somehow magically abandon your coffin and are now floating above the clouds. He is convinced you are doing well because now you're an angel and can eat clafoutis aux cerises up there every day. You adored that warm cherry cake, didn't you?

I recently fixed him spaghetti and his favourite sauce (a little ketchup combined with cream and everything warmed up in a pot – I can still manage that), and as I did so, Arthur suddenly announced that you'd told him you were going on a very, very long trip, and that you wouldn't be able to get phone calls where you were going because the reception was so bad.

'But don't worry, Papa,' he added. 'We'll see each other there someday, and until then, Maman will visit us in our dreams. She said she would. I often see her in my dreams,' he assured me, though I wasn't completely sure that he wasn't just making this up to help me feel better. 'She looks like an angel, and has long hair now.'

Yesterday, he also wanted to know if you had wings and if you really could see EVERYTHING from heaven. I think he'd secretly eaten some chocolate after brushing his teeth and was a little anxious about that.

I wish I could cope with your death as well as Arthur has, Hélène. Now and then he's sad and misses his Maman, but he has been much quicker at accepting that you no longer exist

*down here. He often asks me what Maman would say to things –
and I wonder that myself. I have so many questions and no
answers, my beloved. Where are you now?*

I miss, miss, miss you!

*I have used only one exclamation mark here, but it ought to be
a thousand.*

*I've grown humble in my pain. I'd be satisfied if I could just
borrow you from 'up there' for one afternoon a month, so we
could spend a few hours together. Wouldn't it be wonderful if
something like that were possible?*

Instead of that, I'm finally writing to you. Anyway.

*I'm glad that Mamie lives so close that she can take care of
Arthur. She helps me so much. She misses you, as well. She liked
you from the start, from the very first time I took you home to
meet her. Remember? She is the complete opposite of the evil
mother-in-law. And like every good grandma, she idolises little
Arthur. He can twist her around his little finger with his endless
chattering, and she can't resist any of his requests. It's enough to
make you jealous. I don't recall her being nearly so patient and
kind with me. When it gets warmer, the two of them want to
drive to Honfleur for two weeks, to the beach. It will do the boy
good to not have to see my mournful expression all the time.*

*Favre showed up at my door this morning. He also came to
the funeral with his wife Matilde, who seems like a very nice,
warm-hearted person. Of course, he wants to know what's going
on with the new novel. I have no idea if I'll ever finish it. You
would tell me that I need to pull myself together, but I still need
some time. Time gives, time takes away. Time heals all wounds.*

That's the stupidest saying I've ever heard.

I can only hope that you are doing better, my angel! By the way, you might be happy to hear that I ordered a marble gravestone for you. It's decorated with a bronze tablet with the head of an angel on it. Alexandre, our super-aesthete, knew of a stonemason who works with a sculptor. He was the one who designed the relief, using a picture of you as the model. Even Arthur recognised you right away when we visited your grave recently. It turned out exquisitely. I told him that the two of us had met at this cemetery, at Heinrich Heine's grave. I explained that without this poet, he might never have been born. That made him laugh out loud.

I'm going to drive to the Cimetière Montmartre tomorrow and deliver my first letter to you. I'm so sorry it took me this long. Now that the curse has been broken, the next will be with you much quicker. And you'll be amazed because I've come up with something very special for our one-sided correspondence.

Until then, my beloved Hélène, until my next letter – until you can be mine again, like once in May.

Julien

2

Everyone needs somewhere they can go

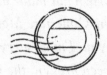

The spring-like sky was playing games with me. As I walked out of the Abbesses Metro station the following morning, it began to pour, causing the young girls trying to take their pictures in front of the belle époque *Métropolitain* sign to scatter like confetti. They shrieked and laughed, and scampered into one of those nearby cafés that are always quite full this time of day.

I took cover in one of the doorways, until the rain let up and I could continue on my way to the Cimetière Montmartre. I absentmindedly reached up to verify that the letter was still tucked in the inside pocket of my brown leather jacket.

Strangely enough, I felt better today than I usually did. Knowing that I'd finally written to Hélène gave me a good feeling, even if it made nothing get better. Had the writing had some kind of cathartic effect? Whatever the case, I didn't wake up last night around 4 a.m., as had become my norm over the past few months. Over time, I had come to detest those early hours, when my thoughts crouched on my chest like evil spirits and the darkness gnawed at my soul.

'What are you doing today, Papa?' Arthur had asked at breakfast, as he gazed at me with interest over his mug of hot chocolate, his hands wrapped around it. He never asks me that. Maybe children really do have 'a nose for things', as my mother likes to say.

I studied his cocoa-smeared mouth and smiled.

'I'm visiting Maman today,' I said.

'Oh, can I come too?'

'No, not today, Arthur. You have to go to nursery school.'

'Pretty please!'

'No, my love, next time!'

Today I had a mission that couldn't be interrupted.

After I dropped Arthur off at nursery school – pitying looks from the nursery-school teachers, since I was the unfortunate man who'd lost his wife prematurely and who got a free pass for running late in the afternoons – I caught the 12 line, which took me through the underground Metro network to Montmartre. Since I lived in Saint-Germain, the cemetery that far north in Paris didn't exactly sit on my doorstep. This distance was perhaps a good thing, otherwise I might have just moved into the graveyard. As it was, each trip through the dark tunnels of the swaying Metro became a short journey at the end of which I emerged into a different world, one that was green and silent.

Here – between the weathered statues, the sunken gravestones draped with the patina of forgetfulness, and the fresh flowers that glowed brightly even while wilting, until their colour faded completely – time hung suspended, as if the earth had ground to a halt.

I automatically slowed my pace as well as I passed through the cemetery gates and trailed along desolate paths, the puddles reflecting the clouds overhead. I followed the Avenue Hector Berlioz for several steps and nodded at the cemetery gardener who passed me, rake in hand, before taking a right turn down Avenue de Montebello. I strode along one of the smaller trails, on the lookout for the large chestnut tree. The flowers would soon be sending their enchanting scents. I instinctively patted my jacket pocket, where the chestnut I'd picked up on the day of the funeral was still nestling. I wrapped my fingers around the shell, which felt so comforting and smooth in my hand, like an anchor.

I glanced to my right, in the direction of Heinrich Heine's grave. It was sitting there, behind a screen of green bushes and gravestones that seemed to merge together in the distance. I could no longer recall what it was that had taken me to the Cimetière Montmartre all those years ago. I practically never went to the 18th arrondissement, one of those quarters that draw so many tourists, thanks to the Sacré-Cœur, the views across Paris, and its charming, winding alleys. It might have been my best friend Alexandre who'd insisted that at least once in life everyone needed to walk through the Cimetière Montmartre, even if for no other reason than to visit the final resting place of Marie Duplessis, the model for Marguerite Gautier, better known as the Lady of the Camellias, immortalised by Alexandre Dumas. On that particular day in May, which felt like an eternity ago, I was strolling through this enchanting cemetery, wandering lost in thought between the angels and the crumbling gravestones, which with their columns and sharply pitched roofs resembled small cottages, in search of the grave belonging to *La Dame aux Camélias.* I never made it there, though, because something else attracted my attention: a head of coppery curls that flared up in the sunshine and floated like a twilight cloud above the gravestones. These curls belonged to a young woman in a green dress, who was standing respectfully in front of the bust of Heinrich Heine and reading the lines of verse that are chiselled into the marble slab set into the ground. She was pressing a portfolio against her chest, and her head was cocked to one side. I fell in love at once with her soft red mouth and pert freckled nose. I quietly walked up beside her, also cocked my head a little, and quietly read the words once written by the German poet who had found his final resting place here:

> Where, for one who is weary of travel,
> will my last resting place be?
> Beneath palms in the south?
> Beneath lindens by the Rhine?
> Will I, somewhere in a desert,
> be buried by a foreign hand?
> Or will I rest by the coast
> of a sea in the sand?
> Still, I will be surrounded
> by God's heaven there as well as here;
> and as funeral lamps,
> stars will float above me at night.

She turned toward me and studied me curiously. She was tall, almost as tall as I am.

'Lovely, isn't it?' she finally said.

I nodded. At the same time, my reading must have left much to be desired, meagre as my German skills are.

'Do you like Henri Heine's poems, too?' She pronounced his name with a French accent, and so tenderly, as if he were a relative: *onri 'äne.*

'Very much,' I lied. I had read next to nothing by this poet before now.

'I love Henri Heine,' she explained fervently. 'One of the last Romantic poets.' She smiled. 'I'm currently writing my master's thesis about him and Romantic irony.'

'Oh, how interesting!'

'The poor man didn't have an easy life. He was sickly and had no homeland, you could say. That's enough to turn you ironic. After all, you have to find some way to save yourself, right? And yet he wrote such wonderful poems.'

She stared pensively at the bust, whose face expressed a touch of misanthropy.

'I'm just glad that he could have his final resting place here, and not under German lindens, where nobody understood him anyway. At least he is united with Matilde here. It was his express wish to be buried here, at the Cimetière Montmartre. Did you know that?'

I shook my head. 'No, but I can understand why. This really is a welcoming spot.'

'Yes,' she agreed absently. 'I would also like to be buried here when I die. I love this cemetery.'

A bird twittered somewhere, and the light filtered down through the trees, painting ripples along the path where we stood beside each other.

'You shouldn't think about death on such a pretty day as today,' I said, having decided to make a risky suggestion. 'Would you maybe like to have a cup of coffee with me? I would enjoy learning more about your friend Heine and Romantic irony.'

'Hmmm. And I'd bet something about me as well, right?' she replied, and shot me an impish glance. It hadn't taken her long to see through me.

I smiled, a little guiltily. 'Mainly about you.'

That is how I met Hélène. At a cemetery. Later, we enjoyed telling the story as a humorous anecdote, but back then, on that day in May as we sat in the sunshine in front of a café, stretching our legs and playfully flirting, I never would have believed it possible that only a few years later I would actually be visiting her here.

By the time I reached Hélène's grave, my feet were wet. Lost in my memories, I'd trudged through a puddle where a few cigarette butts were disintegrating.

A fresh bunch of forget-me-nots lay in front of the pale, narrow gravestone with the bronze relief of the angel's head in profile, the one with Hélène's features. Who could have left these?

I glanced around but didn't see anyone. I plucked a few chestnut leaves from the green ivy that covered the grave, stood back up, and let my gaze drift sadly across the plain marble block on which Hélène's name and life dates were engraved in golden sans serif letters. Under these were three lines that would always remind me of our first meeting:

Come, my love,
be mine again
Like once in May.

Someday we would once again have each other. I'm not a pious man, but there was nothing I longed for more than this. Perhaps we would one day dance together as white clouds, perhaps we'd be entwined in an eternal embrace as the roots of two trees. Who knew?

'Hélène,' I whispered. 'Are you doing well?'

I gently brushed my fingers across the angel's face, and my throat tightened. I swallowed. 'Look, I kept my promise. Now, just watch.'

I pulled the letter from my jacket and glanced around one more time before kneeling to reach out and feel around for a certain spot on the lower reverse side of the gravestone. When I pushed the button, it triggered a mechanism that opened a compartment built into in the stone but invisible to the casual observer. The cavity inside it was large enough to hold the thirty-three letters that would be preserved here for eternity. The stone flap opened. I quickly stuck the envelope inside and pressed it shut again.

No one but my beautiful angel, lost in reverie and gazing ever outwards, and the stonemason who had fulfilled my request and whom I would never meet again, would ever know about the little compartment that I'd had made for my letters to Hélène. I was very proud of this idea that enabled me to place my correspondence in a secret mailbox and to bring them to so intimate a place.

Everyone needs somewhere they can go when they need to visit a dead person, I thought. This desire might explain why we even have cemeteries. You could certainly set up a photo with a candle beside it, but that wasn't a real place. Not the place where the beloved person was sleeping.

A quiet rustling startled me and I turned and looked around the graveyard to see a marmalade cat spring out from behind a crumbling gravestone in pursuit of a leaf that the wind had torn from the tree. I laughed in relief. I hadn't told anyone about Hélène's unusual last wish. Not even Alexandre knew about the letters.

A few minutes later I headed towards the cemetery gate. I was watching the ground as I walked, and almost collided with a woman hurrying down one of the winding paths that led to the gate. It was Cathérine.

'Cathérine! What are you doing here?' I said.

'The same thing as you, I'd guess,' she replied sheepishly. 'I was at the grave.'

'Yes, well . . . me, too,' I admitted lamely.

We were both self-conscious for some reason, and seemed to have no idea what to say next. Running into someone at a cemetery wasn't quite the same as meeting them in a café or in the apartment corridor – maybe people prefer to be alone when they are sad.

'It turned out nicely, the gravestone,' she finally said. 'Truly lovely. Especially the angel.'

I nodded. 'Yes.' And just to have something else to say, I asked: 'Were you the one who left the forget-me-nots?'

She nodded. 'I found a few old flowers there, but they were all wilted. I hauled them off. I hope that was all right. The rain . . . ' She shrugged apologetically.

'Sure, that was just fine.' I smiled.

I didn't want to make it seem as if I wielded absolute control over what happened at Hélène's grave. After all, anyone could visit any grave they wanted. The dead in Montmartre couldn't prevent strangers from coming to their graves to leave flowers or take pictures. Besides, Cathérine had been Hélène's friend.

'Did you take the Metro here? Would you like to go back together? Or go somewhere for a cup of coffee? I have no class this morning.' She tucked a strand of hair behind her ear and looked at me with that mournful gaze.

'I'd like that another time. I have to meet someone shortly. Alexandre,' I quickly said, and it wasn't a lie this time.

'All right . . .' she remarked, then seemed to hesitate. 'Are you . . . uh . . . doing okay, more or less?'

'More or less,' I said shortly.

'You know you can bring Arthur down whenever you want. He likes to play with Zazie.' She attempted a smile. 'We could have supper together some time. I'd cook something nice for us. I know you've been through a hard time, Julien. We all . . .' Her half-moon eyes glittered, and I was afraid she would break down in tears any second.

'I know. Thank you, Cathérine. I really have to go now. Take care . . .'

I threw her an indefinite gesture that could mean anything, and made my escape. It wasn't very polite of me, but I left her standing there and could feel her disappointed eyes gazing after me, as I disappeared into the bustle of the busy streets surrounding the Place des Abbesses.

3

No man should be on his own for long

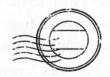

'Old man, you look done in,' Alexandre said. 'Are you eating these days, or just smoking?'

I shook my head. 'Thanks for the support, Alexandre. That's what I like about you.'

I risked a quick glance into the old Venetian mirror hanging to the left of the shop door. I really did look remarkably grey. My full, slightly wavy hair was a little too long, and the rings beneath my eyes were spectacular.

'It might be hard to believe, but today's felt like one of my better days,' I sighed, trying to smooth my hair.

I had recently started categorising my days as good, better and bad ones, even though there hadn't been any good ones yet.

'Huh, really? I wouldn't have guessed that.' Alexandre held a signet ring in pink gold up to the light and nodded contentedly. He then slipped the ring into a little dark blue velvet bag, before eyeing me critically.

'Tell me . . . Do you ever wear anything except that grey turtleneck?'

'What do you have against my sweater – it's cashmere!'

'True, but have you made a vow or something? I'm going to wear this sweater until the trumpets of Jericho blow?' He raised his eyebrows and grinned. 'Every time I see you, that's what you're wearing.'

'Bullshit. Besides, you don't see me all the time.'

I was standing in Alexandre's shop on the Rue de Grenelle, and I was already feeling better, like every other time I was with him. Alexandre was the only person in my circle of acquaintances who treated me completely 'normally'. He never took into account 'my situation', and even though his lack of sympathy sometimes annoyed me, I always knew that his surliness was just for show.

Alexandre Bondy was one of the most empathetic people I knew, an artistic soul with crazy ideas and delicate manual skills. He was my closest friend, and he would have sacrificed his right arm for me if necessary. When we were younger, we used to go skiing together every winter in Verbier or Val d'Isère, and had a blast. We always pretended to be brothers who looked nothing alike, he with his black hair and dark eyes, I with my dark blond hair and blue eyes. We called ourselves Jules and Jim. Of course, I was Jules and he was Jim, in keeping with the characters' appearances. However, fortunately, we never fell in love with the same woman, like the heroes in the film. For my thirtieth birthday, Alexander gave me a watch with 'Jules' engraved on the back, executed by himself.

Alexandre was a goldsmith, one of the most creative and expensive in Paris. His small shop bore the name 'L'espace des rêveurs', The Dreamers' Space. I didn't know of a single woman who hadn't fallen instantly in love with his exquisite handcrafted jewellery. Some of his pieces were ornamented with tiny precious stones in pale spring colours, while others were studded with plump, gleaming, black South Sea pearls, which must be pretty rare if the price tag was any indication. Round or angular pendants of hammered matte gold or silver engraved with quotes from Rilke or Prévert. Shimmering pointy fairy hearts out of rose quartz, agate or aquamarine in golden, cross-shaped settings, a pinhead-sized ruby at their intersection. No one I knew was more detail-obsessed than Alexandre. Every three months he had his shop painted a different colour – maybe dark grey, linden green, burgundy – and along the walls, hand-fired square ceramic tiles in milky white were mounted. In his fine black cursive, he would write sentiments in the middle of each one, such as *flower dust* or *chagrin d'amour* or *kingdom* or *Toi et moi – you and I*.

Anyone who could create and design such enchanting objects must be extremely sensitive, and I believe that there was nobody at this time who knew as much as Alexandre about what was going on in my heart and mind. He was a true friend, but he hated platitudes and spared me well-meaning sayings like 'Time heals all wounds' and 'It'll get better.'

That was the problem right now. Nothing was getting better. I couldn't find consolation, at least not yet.

'I was just at the cemetery,' I said.

'Great, then you must be hungry. Fresh air always makes one hungry.'

He gently set the velvet bag in the gigantic, dark grey safe that loomed against the shop's back wall. He shut the heavy steel door and punched in a code.

33

I nodded and was amazed to realise that I actually was hungry. The croissant I'd carelessly dunked in my coffee this morning hadn't lasted long.

'Let me quickly put a few things away, and then we can go. Gabrielle should be here any minute.'

He vanished into the shop's back room, and I could hear him clattering around with his tools. Unlike me, Alexandre is extremely fastidious. Everything has to always be in its place. Disorder causes him almost physical pain. I walked over to the door, lit a cigarette, and watched for Gabrielle.

Gabrielle Godard was a slender, pale creature with dark hair that she always wore up, just like she always dressed in black or white garments and wrote out all receipts by hand, dark blue ink on creamy handmade paper. She was the secret queen of L'espace des rêveurs. With inimitable grace, she wore the jewelry that Alexandre created, and she made sales without being a sales clerk. She was his muse and, I suspected, the secret queen of his heart. I didn't know this for a fact, but the two of them would fit together perfectly, in light of their eccentricities and their sense of style.

Gabrielle was taking her time, so I stubbed out my cigarette and went back inside. I walked around the illuminated vitrines that lined the currently sky-blue walls, admiring the displays. One ring in particular caught my eye. It looked like it was made of spun gold. Very fine golden strands wrapped around and around each other until they formed a heavy gold ring, worthy of a medieval queen. I had never seen anything like it. Obviously a new model.

'So, do you like my strand ring?' Alexandre asked proudly, as he straightened his black glasses. 'My newest creation. Naturally, it can also be ordered with diamonds or rubies worked into it.'

'A masterpiece,' I acknowledged appreciatively. 'As if spun by the lovely miller's daughter herself.' I sighed. 'It's a shame I no longer have need for something like that.'

'Yes, a real shame,' he agreed bluntly. 'However, you should feel good about the fact you've saved a ton of money. This piece would cost you quite a bit more than the gold from the lovely miller's daughter.'

'That's small consolation.'

'I'm just saying. Come on, let's go and eat! I don't want to wait any more.'

Just as we were about to leave the shop, Gabrielle fluttered toward us in her black feathery clothes. After a subdued greeting, she swept past us through the door and took up her position. A short time later we were sitting at the crowded bar in Alexandre's favourite *traîteur* on the Rue de Bourgogne, and eating chicken with cooked chicory in a red wine sauce. Alexandre didn't have to push me to share a bottle of Merlot with him. We chatted about this and that, just not about Hélène, and as the pleasant warmth of the wine spread throughout my body, life seemed to shift briefly back to 'normal'. I listened to Alexandre's stories, tearing off a piece of fresh baguette from time to time to lazily drag through the peppery sauce.

The food was simple and good.

Alexandre wiped his mouth with his napkin.

'And? How's the writing going?'

'It's not,' I answered honestly.

He inhaled disapprovingly and shook his head a couple of times.

'You need to start pulling yourself together, Julien.'

'I can't. I'm too unhappy.' I drained my glass and felt a surge of self-pity wash over me.

'Don't start crying now,' Alexandre ordered, though I could feel his concerned look. 'Most of the great writers were at their best when they hit rock bottom. Just think about . . . Fitzgerald or Yeats, or . . . Baudelaire. Great despair can sometimes catalyse an insanely creative impulse.'

'That's not happening to me, idiot. My publisher expects an outrageously funny novel from me, a com-e-dy.' I stared at my wine glass, which by now was unfortunately empty.

'So what? All good clowns are deeply sad creatures.'

'That may be, but I'm not performing in a circus, where someone might accidentally dump a whole bucket of water over their head or slip on a banana skin. What I do is a little more demanding.'

'You mean, what you're *not* doing.' Alexandre gestured at the huge waiter behind the bar and ordered two espressos. 'And now what?'

'No clue. Maybe I should just walk away from writing.'

'How would you earn a living?'

'Doing something that requires a limited vocabulary,' I shot back cynically. 'I could go into ice-cream sales. I'll purchase an ice-cream maker and a cart, and then . . . Vanilla, chocolate, strawberry . . .'

'Marvellous idea. The sad ice-cream man from Boulevard Saint-Germain. I can see it now. People will come running, just to see your melancholy face.'

With his huge hands, the giant set our tiny demitasse cups of thick porcelain on the counter and slammed a sugar shaker down next to them.

'What should I do? I lack inspiration.'

'Do you want my opinion?' Alexandre stirred some sugar into his coffee.

'No, I don't.'

'What you lack is a woman.'

36

'Right. I lack Hélène.'

'But Hélène is dead.'

'It might be hard to imagine, but I've noticed that.'

'Now you're pissed off.' He slipped his arm placatingly around my shoulders. I shook him off.

'That's enough, Alexandre. You're insensitive.'

'No, I'm not. I'm just your friend. And I'm telling you, you need a woman. No man should be on his own for long. That's just not good.'

'I didn't ask for this, okay? I was very happy.'

'That's exactly the point. You *were* happy. And now you're obviously not. It's all right to admit that.'

I let my head sink into my hands.

'I admit everything. And now what?'

'*Now* . . . is always the right time because it's the only time.'

'You should hear yourself. You sound like a priest,' I replied gloomily.

'All I mean is that you need to rejoin the human race. You're thirty-five years old, and you've spent the past six months living like a hermit – Julien!' He gently shook me, and I lifted my head out of my hands. 'I'll be opening my spring exhibition the Saturday after Easter, and I want you to come. Maybe you'll rediscover your inspiration there, who knows? A little human society will do you good, my lad.'

He drained his espresso in one gulp and abruptly grinned at me. 'Did you know that unhappy young widowers rank quite high when it comes to women?'

'I don't care.'

'The same goes for unhappy *old* widowers, but only if they're very rich. Maybe you should write a few more bestsellers and save the ice-cream idea for your next life.'

'Stop, Alexandre!'

'*Bon*, I'll stop. I have to get back to the shop anyway.' He glanced at his watch, which matched mine. 'But you have to promise that you'll come.'

'I promise, though under duress.'

'That doesn't matter. We can't always do what we'd like to.'

Alexandre tossed a few notes onto the bar, and we walked out and said goodbye.

Easter was two weeks away, and my mother was planning to take Arthur to the beach for fourteen days. Once they'd left, I'd be able to visit Alexandre's exhibition without having to make major arrangements. The party might actually help distract me. At any rate, it was a date in the calendar of my otherwise monotonous and joyless life, whose days were all running together, all shaped by the same rhythm of sleeping, eating, taking Arthur to nursery school, and picking him up from nursery school.

I really did plan to go to the spring exhibition. I even wrote the date, 17 April, in my planner, although I was worried that I might not know anyone there. I'd never been good at making small talk.

The fact that I ultimately didn't go to Alexandre's party was related, though, to a different matter, one that would send me into deep confusion.

4

King Arthur of the Round Table

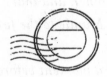

My Most Beloved Darling,

Last night, Arthur suddenly appeared like a little ghost in the bedroom door. He was crying bitterly, and Bruno, his old brown teddy bear, was dangling from his hand. I switched on the bedside lamp and jumped up in alarm. I sleep very lightly now that I'm the only one in our bed. I no longer sleep like a log, the way you used to tease me about whenever you'd sweep back the curtains to let the sun in.

I crouched down next to our little boy and wrapped my arms around him.

'Pumpkin, what's wrong? Do you have a tummy ache?'

He shook his head and just kept sobbing. I picked him up and carried him and the bear, clutched tightly against his chest, to our bed. I tried stroking his wet little face and calling him all the pet names I could think of, but it took him an age to come round.

'No, leave me alone! Maman's supposed to come. I want Maman to come!' he suddenly cried out, beating his little legs against the coverlet.

I watched him, helplessly. I could've given him anything in the world he wanted, just not this.

'Pumpkin, Maman's in heaven. You know that,' I said quietly and unhappily. 'We'll both have to manage without her for a while. But we have each other, and that's something, isn't it? And on Sunday we'll go with Mamie to the Jardin des Plantes, and visit the animals.'

The sobs broke off for a moment before starting up again.

I spoke gently with him and talked imploringly, like a priest reciting the sacrament. Through his tears and hiccups, he told me at last that he'd had 'a bad dream'. And it really was a nightmare, Hélène. It shamefully revealed to me that Arthur, our cheerful, vivacious little Arthur, who had seemingly made his peace with the new situation and who'd tried so hard to cheer up his mournful father, hadn't coped with the death of his Maman as completely as I'd thought. It may be true that children adapt to new situations more easily than we adults, but what other choice do they have? I have heard Arthur talk to his friends at nursery school about you with such great naturalness, about things that we adults never vocalise. It always reminds me of that old film of René Clément's – Les jeux interdits, Forbidden Games – that we watched together in the little theatre in

Montmartre. You liked the score so much that you later bought a CD of that Spanish guitarist, Narciso Yepes, and listened to it over and over again. I still recall how touched we were by that film. We sat there all the way through the credits, mutely holding hands. I think we were the last people to leave the theatre. Little Paulette and her friend Michel – as they coped with the war in their childish way, playfully dealing with the death and horror that surrounded them, and creating their own world which had its own order and meaning. Do you recall how they stole all the crosses from the cemetery and even out of the church in order to create graves for Paulette's dead dog and all the other dead animals in their secret graveyard? I have always thought that children are amazing creatures, with the way they can slip into fantasy, and the simplicity and clarity with which they view things. The way they live their lives and how they somehow make things work out for the best for them. When do we lose this – our faith in life itself?

Arthur's dream also took place in a cemetery. I still feel a chill when I think about it. He was all alone at the Cimetière Montmartre, as he explained. At first we were walking down the path together, but then he got distracted for a moment and I was suddenly gone. So he searched for your grave, hoping to find me there. He wandered around the graveyard for hours and got lost, stumbling down paths and allées, weeping and calling for me. He finally found it, your grave. A man in a leather jacket was standing in front of the gravestone with the angel's head, and Arthur was so relieved.

He called: 'Papa! Papa!'

But when the man turned around, it was a stranger.

'Who are you looking for?' the strange man asked nicely.

'I'm looking for my Papa!'

'What's your Papa's name?'

'Julien. Julien Azoulay.'

'Julien Azoulay?' the stranger asked, before pointing at the gravestone. 'Yes, this is where he is. He died a long time ago.'

And suddenly there on the gravestone wasn't just your name, but also mine, as well as Mamie's and even Cathérine's and her cat Zazie's. And just like that, he knew that everyone was dead. He was all alone in the world.

'But I'm only four,' he sobbed, staring at me with his big eyes, panic-stricken. 'I'm only four!' He unhappily held up his hand and showed me four fingers. 'I can't be on my own.'

My heart twisted in my chest.

'Arthur, pumpkin, that was just a dream. A bad dream, but none of it is true. You aren't alone. I'm still here. I'm always here, trust me. I'll never leave you, so don't worry about that.'

I took him in my arms and rocked him back and forth softly. I spoke calmly to him until his sobs gradually faded away.

That dream made me feel sick, Hélène, and Arthur's fears and his childish despair cut me to the quick. I comforted our little one as best I could. My conscience pained me, and I swore to take better care of Arthur from now on. I'll read books to him, watch films with him. I'll take him to the Tuileries to eat waffles and sail little white boats across the big lake. I'll take him out to the country and go for walks along meandering streams. In the summer we'll go for picnics in the Bois de Boulogne, spread our blanket underneath some shady tree and stare up at the sky. I'll even take him to that dreadful Disneyland he talks about all the time for his fifth birthday. I'll let him bring a few friends along, and we'll hurtle down the Wild West roller coaster and follow that up with mountains of French fries and cotton candy. I will try to focus less on myself and to be more of a committed father. Yes, I will even try to write, even if it might only be a page a day.

'Papa, can I sleep with you tonight?' he finally asked.

'Of course, pumpkin, the bed is big enough.'

'Could you leave the light on, too?'

'Sure.'

He was asleep a few minutes later. He gripped my hand tightly and had Bruno squeezed under his other arm.

Did you know, Hélène, that back around the time of your funeral, he asked me if he should give you Bruno to take along on your trip? 'Then Maman won't be so alone,' he said, and hugged his bear as he looked at me, uncertainly.

It would have been a huge sacrifice.

'That's a great idea, Arthur,' I said. 'But I don't think Maman is quite that fond of teddy bears. Bruno should stay with you.'

He nodded, relieved.

'You're right,' he said, then paused for a moment. 'What if I give her the red knight and my wooden sword?'

That is how his favourite knight, and the sword he spent so long picking out at Si tu veux, that magical toy shop in the Galerie Vivienne, made their way into your coffin, darling. No idea if you actually have a use for them where you are. Arthur said that a sword can always come in handy.

As I lay next to him last night – this all happened around three – I spent a long time studying his tender face with its dark eyelashes, in the glow from the bedside lamp. He is still so little, a baby bird, and I vowed to protect his fragile spirit with all the strength I have. I so wish I could shield him from all the bad things in the world.

I watched that sleeping child, for whom I would sacrifice my life, and thought how he'll soon grow bigger. He'll pull pranks with his friends, get a five in maths (if he has inherited my genes, that is), listen to ear-splitting music in his room from which I will be banished, go to his first concert with friends. He'll stay out all night long until the sun appears as a pink streak across the sky, will fall in love for the first time, will drown his relationship sorrows and tears while ripping a picture of a pretty girl into a thousand little pieces. He will make mistakes and get things just right. He will be sad, as well as ecstatically happy, and I will stay at the side of this marvellous little boy as long as I possibly can. I will help him and watch him grow and grow up, and become the finest possible version of himself.

And one day, he will be the one at his father's side.

I gave Arthur a kiss, and for a fleeting moment, I was overcome by the thought of how thin the ice is that we move on when we pin our hearts on something living.

We are all so fragile. Every day. Every hour.

I remember us discussing names for him. At that point, he was just a cloudy shape on the ultrasound scan in your hand.

'Arthur – isn't that a big name for such a little creature?' I'd

asked. Arthur made me think about the knights of the Round Table. 'Why not just Yves or Gilles or Laurent?'

You laughed. 'But, Julien, he won't stay small for ever. He will grow into his name, you'll see. I like Arthur, an old name with a nice sound.'

And so we stuck with Arthur. Arthur Azoulay. What will become of our little knight of the Round Table? We'll have to see. It's a shame you're no longer here to watch your little son grow into his name. We thought that was going to go differently, didn't we? But maybe, maybe, maybe you can still watch everything with your lovely eyes which have closed for ever.

I do so hope that. I will take good care of him, I promise.

The world was back in order this morning. Arthur was quite cheerful, and he gulped his breakfast. It was as if that bad dream never happened. Children forget so quickly. Nonetheless, he would like to sleep 'in Maman's bed' all the time now. Then I won't be so alone, and besides our bed is much cosier, he explained. We left at that point, and he happily skipped down the street in his blue rubber boots with the white dots. He'd remembered by then that today was the nursery-school field trip to the puppet theatre in the Parc des Buttes-Chaumont. You know how much he loves the puppet theatre.

On the other hand, I felt completely wiped out, after getting less than three hours of sleep. I may take a nap later on. Luckily, I have no major commitments for the rest of the day. Mamie invited me over for lunch, though. She insisted on it. Her quarrelsome sister Carole will also be there with her husband, the one with dementia. I'll get to watch my own puppet performance. The scenes between the three of them are really absurd and always very entertaining.

There you go! A square meal and a short walk along the Rue de Varenne will do me good.

I sometimes think it would be easier if I had a nine-to-five job, off to the office in the morning and coming back home in the afternoon. The days would pass quicker if I did, since I'd be forced to get something done. As it is, I have to manage my own time, and that's not always easy. It's good that I have to take Arthur to nursery school in the mornings. There's no telling what time I'd wake up if I didn't have to do that.

I often think wistfully about how we used to drink our first cup of coffee together in bed, before you woke Arthur and headed to the nursery. I used to take it for granted when you rejoined me in bed with our two large cups in hand. But today, I miss that quiet fifteen minutes before the day got started and life took over again. That's not all I miss.

Since you've been gone, Hélène, the early morning is my favourite time of day – those few precious seconds before I'm fully awake.

I press my face into the pillow and listen, half-asleep, to the sounds that drift up from the street. A car driving by. A bird chirping. A door slamming. A child's laughter. Just for a moment, all is right in my world.

I reach for your hand, murmur 'Hélène' and open my eyes.

And then reality sweeps over me again.

You are gone, and nothing is the way it should be.

I miss you, mon amour. How could I ever stop missing you?

I will love and miss you – until you can be mine again, like once in May.
From my heart to yours,
Julien

I will love and miss you beyond our long lifetime again. I'll
wait for you...
I'll always wait for you...

Julien

5

Confit de canard

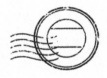

My parents had a happy marriage. My mother, Clémence, was without a doubt the prettiest girl in the sleepy town of Plan-d'Orgon in
the South of France. She grew up in a country hotel, surrounded by
chickens and meadows, as well as hotel guests who either spent their
vacations here or merely stopped off for the night on their way to the
cities and towns of Provence nestled amidst their lavender fields. Les
Baux-de-Provence with its defiant fortress, painterly Roussillon glowing
in the setting sun inside its ring of ochre and reddish cliffs, Arles with
its famous arena and its lively farmers' markets where you could find red
artichokes, black olives and bright fabric balls, or Fontaine-de-Vaucluse
where a stroll along the riverbank offered alluring views into the clear
turquoise depths of the mountain runoff.

If my father hadn't booked a room in this hotel and been smitten by the eyes of the young woman in the pale flowered dress as she floated around the breakfast room like a luminous creature, carrying coffee, croissants, salted butter, goat's cheese, pâté de campagne provençale and lavender honey to the guests, Clémence never would have left her hometown and would have eventually taken over the hotel from her parents. But as it turned out, she moved to Paris with Philippe Azoulay, an ambitious diplomat fifteen years her senior. During the early years of their marriage, she travelled extensively with him until Philippe took a position in the Ministry of Foreign Affairs on the Quai d'Orsay. They moved into an apartment on the Rue de Varenne and had a little boy – me. By that point, my mother was already thirty-four, and my father almost fifty. The birth proved difficult, which was why this child, which the couple had longed for so much, remained an only child.

Despite all the years spent in the big city, Maman never lost her healthy appetite. She is a passionate, accomplished cook, and her love of nature is anchored firmly in her heart. Even though Paris offers no lavender fields or wildflower meadows scattered with poppies and daisies, she loves to roam through the Tuileries or the Bois de Boulogne, because she 'needs to see something green'. She always says it helps soothe her spirits.

Years ago, she made frequent weekend trips out to the country to visit her older sister Carole. Since her husband Paul had grown sick and the two of them had moved to the city to be closer to better medical care, the sisters were now constantly at loggerheads. One impetus for this is Paul's dementia. In his confused state, he believes my mother is his actual wife, which has led to all sorts of wild speculations and jealousy on Carole's part. Also, the older sister is all the more jealous of the younger one because my mother has supposedly had an easier life, all in all, and has been well provided for since the death of my father. Our summer house in Normandy has been a particular thorn in her side for years.

When my father died several years ago, after contracting a lung infection that weakened him to the point he couldn't even stand on his own, my mother inherited the apartment on the Rue de Varenne, as well as the small holiday home in Honfleur, where we had always spent my longer holidays.

The summers had lasted for ever – or at least, that's how they seem to me today. They were redolent of pines and rosemary, and I loved that one-of-a-kind fragrance that floated in the air when you ran through the scrubby bushes and low-growing trees on your way to the beach, the dried wood and branches cracking quietly under your feet.

This was the scent of my childhood, which had been as light and cheerful as those irretrievable summers. The silvery, glittering Atlantic, the fish soup served on evenings down at the harbour, the return home along shadowy country roads, my father at the wheel chatting quietly with my mother while I sat in the back seat of our old Renault, my head resting against the window, drowsy and filled with the feeling of absolute security.

I can still remember clearly the late breakfasts on the shady terrace with its weathered, wisteria-covered wooden trellis: Maman, barefoot, in her white batiste nightgown, with a shawl pulled over it; Papa, never wearing anything less than proper attire, in his blue-striped shirt, light-weight trousers and soft leather shoes. I don't think it would have ever occurred to him to wander through town in shorts and sandals, the typical tourist garb you see everywhere these days. He simply wouldn't have found it elegant enough. He also never would have had breakfast in bed, even though he sometimes carried a steaming cup of café crème to his wife. She, on the other hand, thought there was nothing lovelier than sipping the day's first cup of coffee before getting out of bed.

You could say that, in many respects, my parents were quite different. And yet they loved each other deeply. The secret to their marriage lay in a tall measure of tolerance, a lively sense of humour, and a marvellous generosity of the heart. I wish that, like Philemon and Baucis, they could have departed this world together in their old age and become intertwining trees, locked in an eternal embrace. Unfortunately, life will keep changing its stories.

On the day my father could no longer stand up in order to dress properly to sit at the table, he died.

He was a truly fine man.

As I walked into the apartment on Rue de Varenne that day, the smell of roasted meat was already wafting from the kitchen.

'Mmmm, that smells delicious,' I said.

'I fixed *confit de canard*. I know how much you love it,' Maman explained with a smile, hugging me tightly. 'Come in, come in!'

I don't know a single soul who greets people as joyfully as Maman. She laughs and beams as she takes a step backward to allow the other person to enter, which makes you feel unbelievably welcome.

After untying her apron, Maman tossed it carelessly across a chair and led me into the salon, where a fire was already flickering in the fireplace and the round table was laid for four.

'Sit down, Julien. Carole and Paul won't get here for a little while.'

We sat down on the green velvet couch in the bay window that faced the street, and she pressed a glass of *crémant* into my hand, before holding out a plate full of toasted bread slices covered with a generous layer of pâté.

'You've lost more weight.' She eyed me concernedly.

'Oh, Maman, you say that every time. If that were true, there'd be nothing left of me by now,' I replied defensively. 'I'm eating like normal.'

She smiled indulgently. 'How's Arthur doing?' she asked. 'Is he excited about our trip to Honfleur?'

'Absolutely!' I took a sip of *crémant*, which rolled down my tongue, cold and sparkling. 'He can't stop talking about your trip to the sea. He's never been to the house.'

'And what about you? Do you want to come up for a few days? A little fresh wind in your lungs would do you good.'

I shook my head. 'No, I'll try to get some writing done. I need to make some headway with this stupid book.'

I shrugged and smiled apologetically, and she nodded, tactful enough not to pry for more information.

'But you're still coming along to the Jardin des Plantes on Sunday, aren't you?' she pressed.

'Of course.'

'How are you filling your days now?'

'Oh . . . I . . . well, with the usual stuff,' I explained vaguely. 'Arthur, housework. Louise came by yesterday to clean, and I went to the cemetery and met Alexandre for lunch afterward. He invited me to come to his spring exhibition.'

I reached for the wine glass and noticed that my hand was trembling. I really needed to focus on getting healthy again.

'Your hand is shaking,' Maman declared.

'Yes. I didn't sleep much last night. Arthur had a nightmare, but he was better again this morning,' I hurried to add.

'And you? How are you doing? Are you getting by?'

She looked at me, and I knew there was no point trying to pull the wool over her eyes. You can pretend all you like to other people, but not to your own mother.

'Oh, Maman . . .' I murmured.

'Oh, my child.' She pressed my hand. 'It will get better. Someday soon. You're still so young, and even you will laugh again. You can't spend your whole life being sad.'

'Hmm.'

'You know how much I cared for Hélène, but when I see you so unhappy, I wish I could just speed time along until you found yourself back in a life that made you happy. And then I think, somewhere out there, there's a girl who can love my Julien.'

She smiled. I knew she meant well.

'Could we talk about something else, Maman?'

'Certainly. Next week, I'm going to drive to Oxfam to donate some old things. How would you feel if we cleaned out your closets?' She said *your closets*, but she actually meant Hélène's.

'I can manage that on my own.' There was no way I would let anyone close to Hélène's closet.

'But you won't do it on your own, Julien.'

'Why should I give her things away? They aren't bothering anyone.'

'Julien.' She looked at me sternly. 'I also lost my husband and was very unhappy afterward, as you recall. But I can promise you that nothing good comes from hoarding memories. Memories make us sentimental, and if you're sentimental you can't move forward. You live backwards. It would be best for you if those clothes disappeared and were serving a good purpose somewhere else. You don't want to turn your apartment into a mausoleum like that crazy Monsieur Benoît, do you?'

I sighed and sensed deep down that she was right.

Monsieur Benoît's wife had been killed in an accident when I was still in school. She had stepped out to cross Boulevard Raspail without taking a careful look both ways – like all good Parisians, it was beneath her to cross at a traffic light or use a crossing. She simply took off across the street, trusting that everyone would hit their brakes in time, but in this case, a car struck her.

Jean, Monsieur Benoît's son, had been a classmate of mine. After school, we sometimes went to his house, knowing that we wouldn't be disturbed there since his father always came home late from work. I can still recall how annoyed I was that nothing could be touched or messed with in his parents' bedroom, which was located on the parterre and led to the small garden where we secretly smoked our first cigarettes. Above all, his mother's mirrored vanity was sacred terrain. Everything on it still sat where it had been on the day of the accident: her brushes and combs, her earrings, her pearl necklace, the glass vial holding the heavy, expensive perfume L'heure bleu, and two theatre tickets that would never be used. The last book she had been reading was waiting on the nightstand, while her slippers sat neatly on her side of the bed and her silk robe hung on a silver hook on the door. And the pale-slatted closet door must have concealed all of the dead woman's clothes.

Nothing changed for years, at Monsieur Benoît's insistence. I remembered clearly how spooky I found that back then, and what I told my mother about that ghost house and my certainty that one day Monsieur Benoît's sorrow would drive him crazy.

Was I really on my way to becoming a professional mourner like that weird old mausoleum keeper everyone pitied and poked fun at?

'All right,' I capitulated. 'Let's get it behind us.'

The doorbell cut off our conversation. Maman walked into the hall and opened the door. The apartment grew noisy the moment Carole and her husband stepped inside. My aunt's deafening voice could have woken the dead. I couldn't help grinning at the sound of her loud voice in the hallway, raised in complaints about the capricious weather and the surliness of Parisian taxi drivers.

A short time later, we were sitting at the table, eating the scrumptious *confit de canard* that Maman served with a lingonberry sauce and a light Burgundy wine.

Even old Paul seemed to be enjoying it. In his dark blue woollen sweater, he was hovering over his plate, awkwardly slicing away at the tender marbled meat that disappeared into his mouth, bite after bite. Before retirement, my uncle had been a professor of philosophy, and he had enjoyed teaching us and his three children quotes from Descartes, Pascal and Derrida. His wife Carole, on the other had, was more practical in nature; she had worked in an accountant's office and had managed their money. It was a real shame that this intelligent man, who could interpret practically any philosophical text and whose motto had been Descartes's three famous words – *cogito ergo sum*: I think, therefore I am – had been suffering from dementia for the past few years.

You had to hand it to Carole: she was always at the side of her increasingly perplexed husband. Thanks to the energetic support of a doe-eyed nurse from Guadeloupe, the two of them could continue living in the Bastille neighbourhood, where they had been able to procure a large, relatively reasonably priced apartment several years ago, before the rents had spiked so sharply. The only problem was that Carole had always tended to be quite jealous when it came to her handsome husband. And she was anything but delighted by Paul's obvious infatuation with the pretty nurse with whom he laughed and flirted all the time.

However, even more egregious was the fact that, in his advancing forgetfulness, Paul had started to believe that my mother was his actual wife. This had been going on for some time, to the great irritation and mistrust of my aunt. Paul had always had a weakness for his sister-in-law Clémence, and recently several arguments had arisen in the heat of which Carole accused her sister of having once had a fling with Paul. Maman would vehemently deny this, snapping that Carole was obviously losing her marbles as well. Phone calls between the two sisters typically ended with one or the other of them hanging up in exasperation. Maman would then call me and gripe about her quarrelsome sister, who frequently ended their conversation with a sulky tirade about her joyless life, which would climax in an accusatory commentary on how good my mother's life was in comparison with her own.

The world's displeasures may not be caused by the fact that people, as Blaise Pascal once perceptively pointed out, don't know how to sit quietly in their rooms, but rather by their tendency to compare themselves with others. Aunt Carole was the best proof of this.

'Carole is on the warpath again today,' Maman would say. Followed by: 'I won't be treated this way. I'm seventy years old, after all. *C'est fini!*' Or: 'My sister caused trouble even when she was a child. She always felt hard done by.' And finally, in a more conciliatory tone: 'But she can also be quite nice.'

And Maman was right about that. Aunt Carole could be *quite nice.* On her good days, she could activate her sense of humour and tell funny anecdotes from the past, like about the time she had gone out dancing with her husband until the early morning hours and had danced so exuberantly that she kicked off her shoes.

Aunt Carole knew all the old family stories, and when she talked about the past, her eyes gleamed. She had moved to Paris before my mother had, and in those early months she had helped her younger sister quite a lot.

Maman had never forgotten that. And one or two weeks later – once their tempers had settled back down – the two sisters would start talking again, fully aware that they were still sisters, just like always. Knowing that at her age Carole wasn't in a position to change her ways and that life with Paul was quite challenging, Maman would invite them over to eat. This was one of those days.

In the meantime, we had reached dessert, a *tarte au citron* that looked as if it had been painted.

'You didn't make that yourself, Clémence, did you?' Carole wanted to know.

'Of course I made it myself,' my mother replied, annoyed.

'Really?' Carole studied the tender meringue atop the lemon crème, and prodded it with her small fork. 'It looks so perfect. I thought you must have bought it from Ladurée.'

'Why do you assume I buy everything from Ladurée?' The tone was sharpening.

I was about to intervene when Carole gave a dismissive wave.

'It doesn't matter. It's marvellous either way.' She turned to Paul, who was sitting beside her, and shouted in his ear: 'You like it too, don't you, *chéri*?'

Paul glanced up from his plate and considered the question for a moment. 'D-delicious,' he said, flashing Maman a smile. 'My wife's a good cook, always has been.'

He contentedly shoved the last forkful into his mouth, chewed distractedly, and didn't notice that Carole's expression was threatening to slide southward.

'*Chéri*, what are you saying?' was the swift response. 'Clémence isn't your wife. *I'm* your wife. Me, Carole!'

He shook his head and chased a few crumbs around his plate. 'N-no,' he declared firmly. 'You're the *sister*.'

Carole raised her eyebrows, while Maman laughed and quickly interjected: 'You're confused, Paul. I was married to Philippe. You and Carole are together.'

Paul's eyes scanned the table for help and came to a stop at me. 'Julien!' he exclaimed, and I nodded.

'It's true, Uncle Paul. You're Carole's husband, not Clémence's.'

Carole and Clémence nodded emphatically.

This much contradiction seemed to provoke the old man. He hurled his fork to the floor, before staring at the two sisters suspiciously and saying: 'You both look like two dumb giraffes.'

Sometimes tragedy has a comical side. We all gazed at each other, trying hard not to laugh.

'I want to go to sleep now,' Paul declared as he tried to stand up from his chair.

Carole soothingly patted his arm.

'He can lie down in the guest room,' Maman offered, but Paul would hear nothing of it.

'No, I want to go to the bedroom, to *our* bedroom,' he cried stubbornly.

'How about you stretch out on the chaise lounge here, Paul?' Maman suggested. 'Then you can still be close to us.'

'All right.' He nodded.

Carole led her husband to a sofa covered in a delicate flowered fabric that stood against the wall, not far from the table. Groaning, he settled onto it and then demanded a blanket, which was immediately brought to him. He closed his eyes in satisfaction.

'It can sometimes be very hard with him,' Carole remarked as she joined us back at the table. 'He's become so unpredictable.'

She went on to tell us a story from a few days ago. That afternoon, a neighbour had dropped by. It was Paul's nap time, and the two women were chatting over coffee in the living room, when the door suddenly swung open. There, with a big smile on his face, stood Paul in nothing except his underwear. He studied Carole's neighbour with curiosity and obviously wanted to be introduced to this pretty, dark-haired woman whom he couldn't seem to recall at the moment.

Trying to maintain her composure, Carole said amiably: 'Look, Paul, we have company. Wouldn't you like to go and put on some trousers?'

At this, Paul looked down at himself and remarked drily that he was *already* wearing trousers.

'I try to take everything with a grain of salt,' Carole concluded, reaching for another slice of lemon tart. My aunt had never been particularly sympathetic when it came to illnesses. 'What else am I supposed to do? Most of the time, he's perfectly calm, and we still have some lovely moments together, even if that's pretty hard to believe. Those are the times I can still see a little of the old Paul.' She shook her head. 'But some days are just terrible. I don't know, maybe part of him can tell something's not right with his mind. All I know is that he can suddenly turn completely unbearable. He told me just a few days ago that everything was going to be destroyed "in there", and that we should just nail everything shut.'

She sighed, and Maman carried in the coffee on a silver tray. As we sipped our *petit café* from the fragile Limoges cups, the conversation returned to more banal affairs.

Aunt Carole had brought me some of my favourite sweets – *calissons d'Aix*, a confection from Provence – and she suddenly pulled out of her large purse a tin of the soft almond slices covered in royal icing, shaped like a weaver's shuttle.

'*Tiens*! I almost forgot! I brought a little something for you. To help your nerves and your sad eyes,' she announced unceremoniously.

'Oh, how nice! Thank you so much,' I replied, taken aback by her thoughtfulness.

I thought about the story Aunt Carole used to tell me about the *calissons*, which had supposedly been invented by the chef of the Duke of Anjou, whose lovely bride's eyes were so sad that he wanted to inspire her to smile with these sweets.

However, when the conversation turned to Maman's upcoming Easter trip to Honfleur with Arthur, Aunt Carole gave a deep sigh, as all thoughts about our fates were relegated to the background.

'You have it good, Clémence,' she declared. 'You can always get away. I can't do that any more.'

'Just stop it. I don't leave town all the time, either,' Maman shot back. 'But you're welcome to come along, Carole. Why don't you check Paul into a short-term care facility for a week? He'd survive it, and a change of scenery would do wonders for you.'

'Oh, I don't know.' Carole shook her head. 'I don't like putting him in a home.'

'I thought so! In a home, where they beat the patients.' A quavering voice suddenly floated over from the chaise lounge, and we turned around in surprise.

'That's just nonsense, Paul!' Carole exclaimed. 'I thought you were sleeping.'

'How am I supposed to sleep with all this chattering?' Paul growled, as he threw back his blanket. 'Come on, it's time to go. I want to go home right now.'

Clémence and Carole exchanged a mute look and rolled their eyes.

'Stay a little longer, Uncle Paul. You just got here,' I interjected, sitting down on the foot of the sofa. 'Would you maybe like some coffee?'

'Yes . . . C-coffee!' Paul nodded, then a spark of memory flared up in his grey eyes. 'How's little Arthur?'

'Arthur's doing well. He'll be going to the coast with Mamie soon, and he's looking forward to that.'

'To the coast. How lovely,' Paul murmured as he leaned back against the seat. He then wrinkled his forehead and stared hard at me as he asked loudly: 'Where is Hélène? Why isn't Hélène here?'

An uncomfortable silence settled over the room.

'Paul . . .' Carole finally replied. 'Hélène is dead.'

In their unvarnished bluntness, the words fell through me like stones.

'What? She's dead, too?' Paul mumbled, his eyebrows shooting upward. He then shook his head in embarrassment. 'Why didn't anyone tell me? Nobody tells me anything!' He gazed at us accusingly.

'But we went to Hélène's funeral. You don't remember that?' Carole tried once more.

'I didn't. I wasn't at any funeral,' Paul declared in a strident voice.

'You were. Last October.'

'October, November, December,' Paul recited, having clearly reached the extent of his mental limits.

'I think we'd better go. He's going a bit downhill,' Carole said quietly. 'Could you please order us a taxi, Clémence?'

Maman nodded worriedly and insisted that Carole take the rest of the lemon tart with her. As the door shut behind the pair, we exchanged glances.

'Well,' Maman remarked. 'We all have our burdens.' She paused for a moment. 'At least Hélène didn't suffer long,' she finally added contemplatively.

I nodded, but that fact didn't comfort me.

6

Cleaning closets

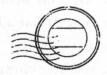

My sadly missed darling,

'At least Hélène didn't suffer long.' That's what Maman said to me just a few days ago when I was at her apartment for lunch. Carole was there, too, along with Paul. Poor Paul is in a fairly pitiful condition. He asked why you weren't there for lunch. He's just getting worse, and this could last for years and years.

Everything went so fast for you, and yet the end still came as a surprise, even though we were expecting it. No, you didn't have to suffer long. The morphine was too good for that. It put you into a coma, and the doctors promised that you'd feel no pain. But I will never know what was going on inside you at the end, what your last thoughts were. There were no famous last words from you, like you see in films when people die.

I sat beside your hospice bed, holding your hand. Your eyes were closed, and you were sleeping, maybe dreaming. The afternoon sun shone brightly through the curtains, while birds chirped outside your window.

At some point, I kissed your forehead and whispered: 'Hélène, darling, I'm going to get some coffee. I'll be right back.'

You moved your head slightly and murmured something inaudible. It could have meant anything. And then – or maybe I just imagined it? – you squeezed my hand gently.

Was that your goodbye? Were the words I couldn't understand 'Take care of yourself' or 'Give Arthur a kiss for me'?

I'd like to think they were.

By the time I returned, you were already gone, my angel, your fragile body only a shape under the white coverlet. Your face was pale and still, your red curls the only spot of colour. Despite all the poison they pumped into you, they remained with you until the end.

And before I realised that everything was finally over, before the pain crashed through me with the fury of a demolition ball and paralysed me for days and weeks, for one short moment, I thought you had finally done it.

I thought that this moment, which had been dangling threateningly over our heads for weeks, had finally reached its fulfilment.

We had said all there was to say to each other, Hélène. We had discussed everything that needed to be and had assured each other of our love so, so often that at least I have a good feeling about that. This knowledge lights my days like a single candle.

Three days before you died, you opened your eyes. A milky haze had already settled across your green eyes.

'My love, come, be mine again, like once in May ...' you whispered, suddenly staring at me in desperate longing. 'Do you still remember, Julien ... in May ... in May ...'

'Oh, Hélène, of course I still remember,' I said. 'How could I ever forget that beautiful day in Montmartre?'

You smiled and sighed quietly, and your eyelids fluttered before closing again. How could I have known that this little exchange would be our last conversation? That these were the final words I would ever have from you?

I was never able to figure out if this sentence came from one of your beloved poems. I couldn't find the verse anywhere. But now it is chiselled into your gravestone, and whenever I see it I am overwhelmed by my certainty that we will meet again some day. But the time will stretch on so long for me, my love!

Maman came over to my apartment yesterday, just as she had threatened. There was no changing her mind. She wanted to clean out the closets with me. Your closets, Hélène! It was strange to see all your clothes, coats and sweaters vanish into the large bags Maman had brought along. All of your colourful scarves and shawls.

I took each piece in my hands and had to give it up. So many small goodbyes!

Now that it's over, I'm very glad I did this 'closet cleaning' with Maman. It is easier when someone is helping you, and you aren't on your own with all the memories. So much of the past crept out of the closet. I saw your clothes and couldn't help recalling situations in which you had worn specific items. I suddenly saw random moments before me, caught like frozen images, things I hadn't thought about in ages.

Eventually, the closets were empty, but no matter how horrible it had been, there was also something liberating about the process.

By the way ... while we were cleaning out your closet and the bureau drawers, we realised just how many red pieces of clothing you owned, Hélène. How bold you were! I don't know of any other redheads who like wearing red as much as you did. Oh, my beloved! Sometimes I sit here writing, and part of me almost expects the door to open. And there you'll be, standing in your red dress with the white polka dots, laughing at me.

I kept your prettiest clothes, and will give them to Aunt Carole for Camille, her youngest daughter. Camille is just as slender and tall as you, and she will love these.

I gave your purses to Cathérine, as well as the silver ring set with the aquamarine, the one you bought that time at the Porte de Clignancourt flea market. She had asked me a few weeks ago if she could perhaps have a personal memento, something of yours she could keep. She was very happy with what I gave her, and wears the ring day and night. She was also very honoured to have your purses, she declared, giving me a sudden, tight hug.

I confess I feel a little uneasy around Cathérine. She is so emotional and sensitive, and I don't deal well with that. She often just brings me down, but I don't want to be unfair. It can't be easy to lose a close friend, either. The two of you did so much together. Can you still recall all those summer evenings when you said you were just going to 'run down quickly' to her place? Your voices, laughing and chatting, would drift up to me all evening from the balcony.

Regardless, Arthur likes spending time with Cathérine. She really has the patience of a saint. They spend hours playing cards, or she reads stories to him from her thick book of fairy tales in which people always end up living happily ever after. Nice idea, right?

The two of them fixed crêpes together last Saturday, and I had to come downstairs to sample everything. It was a lovely afternoon. Arthur's face was bright red, and he was in high spirits because, with Cathérine's help, he had actually managed to flip a crêpe in the air. He was as pleased as punch.

Cathérine told a couple of great stories about you, ones I didn't know, and we laughed and laughed.

Did you really wander around the 10th arrondissement one evening with her, half drunk, looking for your car, which you couldn't find because the police had impounded it hours before? You never told me about that. What other secrets did you keep?

I actually like Cathérine, but the fact that she was such a good friend of yours makes it difficult for me. She was your friend, not mine. I can sense how hard she's trying for Arthur and me, and I suspect she wants to establish the same kind of familiarity that existed between the two of you. The reality is that her attempts make me uncomfortable. I sometimes wonder if perhaps you asked her to take care of us. Even though you're no longer here, chérie, I think I can still feel your influence everywhere I look.

*For example, I found an envelope in one of your handbags
that was stuck right at the back of your closet – I'm just glad I
thought to look through them before giving them to Cathérine.
Most of them didn't have anything interesting in them – two
torn movie tickets from Studio 28, a restaurant receipt, a comb, a
few coins, a piece of gum, a set of photo-booth pictures showing
you and Arthur clowning around. And suddenly in your evening
handbag, I found a mauve envelope with my name on it.*

*I didn't recognise it right away, and my heart pounded in my
ears as I extracted the handwritten note and unfolded it. I found
a poem from Heine, a few short verses, and a sweet saying. And
then I finally remembered discovering that envelope on my desk
after the first time you'd come over to my place. Before that day,
we hadn't even kissed, but one thing led to another. And that
hopeful little poem inspired me to dance around the room in
delight. It made me just as happy as it now makes me sad. And
yet – I was still so glad to have that sign from you!*

The Homecoming

We drove all night long
In the dark post coach;
Our hearts touched,
We joked and laughed.
But when morning broke,
My dear, weren't we amazed!
Between us sat Amor,
The blind passenger.

I wonder how the letter made its way into your handbag. Maybe you were keeping it there for me – for a day like this one, when I would be cleaning out the closets.

I kiss you tenderly, my heart's love, and am grateful for those wonderful, untroubled days that are now light-years away. And yet they seem within arm's reach right now. Oh, to only have you again, like once in May!

Julien

7

The woman in the tree

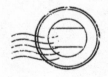

This was the afternoon I met Sophie.

It was the Thursday before Easter, and Arthur had only a half-day of nursery school. He insisted on coming to the cemetery with me, since he was leaving with Mamie the following day.

We ate around noon and then packed his small travel bag, so we didn't make it to the cemetery until after four. Arthur was proudly carrying a rose that we had bought together, along with an Easter arrangement from Au nom de la rose, a small flower shop on Rue Lepic that had caught my eye when I had strolled along Rue des Abbesses.

He was so excited about his trip, and hummed quietly. On the other hand, my heart grew heavy and my spirits flagged the closer we drew to Hélène's grave.

A gentle breeze softly rustled the leaves in the old chestnut tree, and sunbeams shimmered along the path. Arthur placed his rose at the headstone, and I set about cleaning up the grave. I sent him off to toss a faded bunch of daisies onto the nearby compost pile, a rectangular enclosure of boards in which other dying flowers and wreaths were withering away.

In any case, Hélène couldn't complain about her grave not being visited enough. Every time I came to the cemetery I found fresh flowers or a bouquet at the grave.

As Arthur dashed off, I quickly pulled the letter out of my pocket, opened our secret compartment, and added it to the other envelopes. I had written 'for Hélène' on this envelope, as well as the number 3 with a circle around it, so that I could keep track of how many letters I'd already written. There weren't all that many as yet. Although writing them was proving to be unexpectedly comforting, I was still far away from the positive turn in my life that Hélène had predicted. I felt quite alone in the world – not just when I spent my evenings sitting in my apartment feeling lost, but when I walked along the streets of Saint-Germain, which had recently taken on the hints of springtime. On sunny days, people sat around the outdoor cafés, laughing and chatting, so cheerful to the outside eye. Life seemed to be starting anew, but I was still grappling with the unfairness of fate. According to Jean Giraudoux, when a person is gone you suddenly feel like you are surrounded by film extras, and there's nothing you can do to change that.

I stood by the grave for a few minutes and carried on a mute conversation with my beautiful angel, while Arthur chased after a colourful butterfly.

'Look, Papa, isn't it pretty?' he called, but I didn't heed his words.

To my shame, I must admit that I was paying absolutely no attention to my son, and when I turned around after a short while, ready to leave, he was nowhere in sight.

'Arthur?' I hurried a short way down the narrow path, scanning everywhere for his blue jacket. 'Arthur?'

I peered between the shrubs, ran past a few graves, and decided to check the wooden compost enclosure in the hope of finding him there. It was all for nothing though, since everywhere I looked, the cemetery was empty. I couldn't help thinking about Arthur's dream about losing me here, and fear clenched its tight fingers around my heart.

It was a large cemetery, and Arthur was only a little boy.

'This can't be happening,' I muttered as I raced back and forth between the graves. 'Arthur,' I cried again, and again even more loudly: 'Arthur!'

Was he hiding somewhere, playing a trick on me? Maybe he would jump out from behind a gravestone any moment with a giggle.

'Arthur, it's not funny. Where are you?'

I could hear my voice growing hysterical. I tried to be systematic about the paths I ran down, checking both sides, but the small figure in his blue jacket was nowhere to be seen.

A cloud skittered across the sun, and suddenly the cemetery took on the appearance of a spooky, shadowy realm in which the stone figures might come to life at any moment. I quickened my pace, rushing past statues whose blind eyes seemed to be watching me, past the dead resting here for eternity, desperate to find my son whom I'd lost due to my own gross negligence.

And then I saw him.

He was standing a short distance off at the foot of a large linden tree. His head was tilted back, and he seemed to be talking to the tree.

What was he doing here? I paused, bewildered, and then drew closer, relieved to have finally found him. Then I heard sudden silvery laughter that seemed to float down from the tree itself.

I stepped nearer, scanning the branches overhead, and heard Arthur say: 'But Maman's angel is the prettiest one here.'

A hearty chuckle rippled down from the branches.

Who was he talking to? Was that a woman up there?

'Arthur! What are you doing here? You can't just run away like that. You scared me horribly,' I admonished, gently gripping his shoulder.

He spun around with a smile.

'This is Sophie, Papa!' he replied, glancing back up.

I followed his gaze, which is when I caught sight of her.

Concealed by the branches, a young woman was sitting astride the wall. She was as delicate as a pixie, and was wearing dark overalls, her black hair carelessly stuffed underneath a small cap. I would have thought she was a boy if it hadn't been for the huge dark eyes that studied me curiously.

'Hello?' I said, moving a step closer.

The heart-shaped face brightened into a smile.

'Hi!' she said. 'Is this your son?'

'Yes.' I nodded a little reproachfully. 'I've been searching for him everywhere.'

'Sorry about that,' she replied. 'I saw him wandering around the cemetery alone, so I called him over here and we ended up chatting.'

She shifted her position on the wall.

'What are you doing up there?' I asked in amazement.

'She fixes angels, Papa,' Arthur explained to me. 'I already told her ours doesn't need any help yet.'

I chuckled awkwardly. 'That's true,' I said. 'In any case, thank you for taking care of Arthur. Who knows where he might have ended up otherwise? The cemetery isn't exactly small.'

'I know,' she said. 'I work here.'

She pulled her leg across the wall and swung them both over my head as if she were on a swing.

'Are you a sculptor or something?' I asked. My neck was starting to grow stiff from looking up.

'Not really,' she answered. 'Wait a minute, I'll climb down.'

She disappeared behind the tree's boughs, and climbed down a ladder that was leaning against the wall. She decided to skip the last three rungs and simply leaped down to the ground, nimble as a cat.

'Sophie Claudel,' she said.

Studying me from under her dark and now slightly skew-whiff cap, which suited her animated face, she extended her hand. Her grip was astonishingly firm for someone so small.

'So, you're a sculptor after all,' I declared with a smile.

'Oh no,' she shot back. 'I'm no great artist like my namesake Camille. I'm not related to her, either, in case that was your next question.'

'What are you then?'

'A stone worker,' she said. 'I restore statues, funerary monuments, pretty much anything made out of stone.' She gestured around the cemetery. 'The Cimetière Montmartre is one of our bigger clients. Some of the statues urgently need new noses, arms, wings . . . ' She grinned and propped her hands on her hips. 'Even stone takes a beating over time, and marble won't last for ever.'

'What is made to last for ever?' I asked.

'No idea. Lovely words, maybe? Your son told me that you write books. Is it true that you're a famous author, Monsieur?' Again that curious look.

My God, what had Arthur told this cheerful stranger?

'Well ... more of an author of light fiction,' I corrected. 'I'm not exactly Paul Claudel.'

'So who are you?'

'Oh, excuse me. Julien. Julien Azoulay. But it's no big deal if you've never heard of me.'

'Do you always hide your light under a bushel?'

'Where else should I keep it?'

'Papa, could we show her our angel?' Arthur begged, obviously bored. 'Come on, Sophie!'

He tugged at her hand.

'Sure,' said the pixie good-naturedly, and I led the way.

A few minutes later, Mademoiselle Claudel was running her fingers across the bronze head and nodding admiringly.

'Lovely work,' she said, walking around the gravestone to give it a craftsman's appraisal. 'This is good-quality marble, and you'll enjoy it for many years.'

All three of us were standing around Hélène's grave, glowing as it was in the setting sun. Sophie's eyes skimmed the golden inscription, and she reached up to fiddle with a strand of hair that had escaped from her cap, evidently embarrassed.

'I'm so sorry,' she finally said. 'I didn't know that ... I mean it wasn't so long ago ...'

'Yes,' I cut in quickly.

She shook her head sadly. 'An accident?'

'No. My wife had cancer.'

'Oh.'

'It all happened very quickly.'

She didn't reply.

'And that ... poem?' she finally asked. '*My love, be mine again, like once in May* – it almost sounds like ...'

'Like what?'

'A death wish?'

'What's wrong with wanting to be with her?' I exclaimed bitterly. 'My life is practically over.'

'You shouldn't even *think* like that, Monsieur!' Her eyes reflected her shock, but her gaze then turned stern. 'You have a little boy.'

'I know.'

'Self-pity is not a solution.'

'I know.' I pressed my lips together, took a deep breath, and closed my eyes for a moment.

When I opened them again, I discovered that a peculiar smile had spread across Sophie Claudel's face.

'I need to gather up my tools, and then we can go and eat at my favourite bistro,' she declared. 'I would like to tell you something, Monsieur Azoulay, about the living and the dead.'

Looking back, I think that if it hadn't been for Arthur's hopeful face, I would have turned down Sophie's invitation, despite the insistent tone in her voice. As it was, we followed the stone worker across the cemetery. I couldn't begin to describe the relief I felt that Arthur had turned up unharmed. Better still if he'd made a new friend. She kept pausing as we walked along, pointing out graves here and there, some of which needed work, others which had particularly lovely features. She explained certain pieces of plasterwork or relief carvings, and finally took us to an especially impressive nineteenth-century bronze statue that was called *La Douleur*. To reach it, we had to walk up a winding staircase that led to the upper part of the cemetery.

The life-sized figure depicted a mournful young woman with slightly parted lips and loosened hair, which flowed down her back and blended into her floor-length garment. Over the many decades and changing seasons, the figure had assumed a greenish-blue patina. The woman was reclining against a giant gravestone, and her pain looked so real that I found myself rooted to the spot.

'This figure is one of my favourites,' Sophie explained.

'Who is it?' I asked. 'Someone famous?'

She shook her head. 'It was commissioned a long time ago by a mother who was mourning her son's death.'

We resumed our walk and eventually reached a small shed close to the gates, where she dropped off her tool bag.

A few minutes later, we were sitting in L'Artiste, a tiny bistro with a red wooden façade, situated about halfway down Montmartre. Tucked away on Rue Gabrielle, it was a cosy restaurant about the size of a living room. It contained tables covered with red tablecloths and walls plastered with vibrant posters and postcards from the belle époque. Hanging above a battered leather bench, a gigantic picture of cats in sunglasses with wine glasses sitting around long tables in a park, as in a Renoir painting, decorated the back wall. Arthur laughed out loud at the sight of it.

Sophie was greeted at once by a bearded man behind the bar, who kissed her on both cheeks.

We sat down at one of the wooden tables at the window. Arthur seemed delighted that something had finally happened. We hardly ever went out to eat. He swung his legs and looked all around the crowded bistro. When it came time to order, he wanted to try the *lasagne à la Bolognaise*, while Sophie ordered a *cuisse de poulet* and I chose the house *boeuf bourguignon* in red wine sauce.

Sophie called out something to the bearded man behind the bar, and after a few minutes, he appeared with a carafe of water and two glasses of red wine.

'How's Gustave doing?' he asked as he set our drinks down and gave Sophie a wink. 'Is everything going well?'

She laughed and rolled her eyes. 'He's made a fuss since catching that cold,' she said. 'I took good care of him, but now he's starting to talk back and boss me around.'

The man grinned. 'I don't think there's anyone out there who can tell you what to do,' he declared before moving on.

I couldn't help a little smirk. Obviously, Gustave was the pixie's boyfriend, but I had to admit that I couldn't imagine anyone bossing her around, either.

Sophie lifted her glass, her sparkling eyes large and dark.

'To life!' she said. And when I didn't react: 'Well?!'

We clinked our glasses, and somehow I felt both good and surreal as I listened to her explain to Arthur how to use a mallet and how to reconstruct a statue's broken nose with an internal rod to help strengthen it. And then Sophie turned back to me. She was interested and unselfconscious. She ate ravenously and asked me a thousand questions, jabbing her fork in my direction whenever she wanted to make a particular point.

Without a doubt, this was one of the strangest evenings I'd experienced in a long time. And what was even odder was the fact that I actually shared my innermost feelings with this stranger with the reckless smile. I never would have thought it possible, but I ended up telling her about Hélène, my loneliness, and the hard time I was having focusing on my work.

We sat there, as if suspended in a bubble, and it was as if all the cards were reshuffled. Sometimes it's easier to talk about things with a stranger than with people you know well and who know everything about you – or think they do.

In any case, I knew nothing about this dark-haired girl who fixed angels, and possibly broken hearts as well, except that she pursued a very unusual craft – the kind you had to learn these days at an academy – and was older than I'd first assumed. I had guessed her age at about eighteen when I'd seen her sitting on top of the wall. In fact, she was twenty-nine.

'And what about you?' I asked as the waiter cleared away our dishes. 'Isn't it extremely depressing to work in a cemetery? How can you stay so cheerful, considering your profession? All of that – I mean being around that all the time – it must get gloomy.'

Sophie shook her head. 'No, it's the very opposite. I value each day I wake up alive, maybe because I'm so aware of how very limited our time is here. We're just in transit, Monsieur Azoulay. Each day might be our last, which is why' – her eyes bored into mine – 'you need to make the most of the day. Make the most of *every* day.'

I waved this off. 'As in that old saying, *carpe diem.*'

She nodded. 'Exactly. Age doesn't lessen its value.'

'I'm not scared of my last day.'

'But you should be, Monsieur Azoulay. Someday you will be old and grey. Your brittle bones will ache, and reading will be a challenge. You'll only understand about half of what anyone says to you. You will shuffle through your neighbourhood, hunched over and always chilly, and you'll feel constantly exhausted by all the living you've done. At that point, you can go ahead and die, as far as I'm concerned, and join your wife in that grave. But not now.'

She looked at Arthur, who was now eating strawberry ice cream and colouring his placemat with a pen.

'That's a lot to look forward to,' I quipped.

'Not really.'

Her eyes took on the same stern look they'd had back in the cemetery. We had probably now reached the time for the promised talk about the living and the dead.

'Listen, Julien! After such a terrible thing, it makes perfect sense if you are down for a while. That is completely normal. But at some point, you have to stop mourning your dead wife. Mourning is a form of love that only creates more unhappiness. Didn't you know that?'

I stared at her in silence.

'Yes. Do you *want* to be unhappy?' she asked impatiently.

'It's not like you go looking for something like that,' I retorted.

'Sure you can!'

'What do you know about this?' I suddenly visualised Hélène's dear face, and shoved my knife and fork together on my plate, a hopeless gesture.

'More than you'd think.' Sophie studied me closely. 'For example, I know that you were just thinking about your wife.'

I lowered my head.

'It's just the way it is, Julien,' she said gently. 'The dead should always have a room in our memory, somewhere we can visit them. But it is important that we leave them in this room and that we shut the door behind us when we go.'

As we said goodbye outside the bistro, she wished me all the best. 'I'm sure we'll see each other around the cemetery. I'll be there all summer. And don't forget what I said.' She turned toward Arthur, who was drowsily hanging on my hand. 'Take care, little one. And have lots of fun with your *grand-mère*! *Au revoir!*'

She walked down the street in her dark overalls and soft sneakers, waving to us one last time before turning down one of the small alleyways that led up Montmartre.

'She's nice,' Arthur said with a yawn. 'Almost as nice as Cathérine.'

I smiled. 'Goodness, someone's sleepy.'

'Not me,' he protested weakly.

I gripped his little hand more tightly and decided that we would take a taxi back home. It was late already.

I looked up into the sky over Montmartre, where the moon drifted forlornly. It was a half-moon, and I wondered if the old man up there missed his other half as much as I did.

8

All kinds of weather

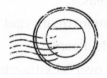

Like everywhere else, April in Paris is a fickle time of year. And my mood shifted just as frequently as the weather over the next two weeks.

After I saw Arthur and Maman off on the train to the Atlantic coast that Friday, I found myself alone for the first time since Hélène's death. I mean, *truly* alone. I unlocked the apartment that was as empty as empty can be, picked up a few of Arthur's Playmobil figures that were strewn across the living-room floor, and suddenly didn't know what I was supposed to feel: relieved to be left in peace to fill my time as I wanted, or abandoned and robbed of the last remaining meaningful structure in my life. For a moment I felt panic-stricken and considered calling Maman to tell her that I would join them at the beach after all. But then the doorbell rang.

This time it wasn't my publisher wondering about the book's progress. It was Cathérine out in the hall, wanting to know if I might like to go with her to Au 35 for a bite to eat. I must confess that I was almost relieved to see her standing there. My refrigerator was empty, and I had no desire to go to the grocery store. To both her and my own surprise, I immediately agreed to go as I pulled my jacket back on.

Au 35 is a small vegetarian restaurant located conveniently on Rue Jacob, number 35, only a short walk from our building. I had been there several times before. The menu was small, and the food good if you liked vegetarian cuisine. Cathérine had given up meat some time ago, since it appeased her conscience.

I wasn't particularly picky that day, and while she ate her sesame quinoa balls and I my *salade au chèvre chaud*, she wanted to know if Arthur's vacation had got off to a good start.

'I'm leaving the day after tomorrow to visit my parents for a few days in Le Havre,' she told me.

It occurred to me that obviously everyone in the building was going to be gone the week after Easter, with the possible exception of Madame Grenouille, who lived on her own in a two-room apartment across the hall from Cathérine. Hélène and I had called her the 'child hater' because she was constantly complaining that Arthur didn't park his little scooter properly in the downstairs entry area. Her eyes gleaming with disapproval, she had never failed to inform us that he was a badly behaved little boy who sang in the stairwell, made too much noise, and bounced his ball too often.

'*Écoutez!* I raised three children,' she would snort whenever Hélène risked contradicting her. 'Every single one of them has better manners than children these days.'

Maybe she had still managed to botch something in their upbringing, since I had never seen even one of her children come for a visit.

'Would you mind feeding Zazie? Only if it's not a bother, though, otherwise I could ask someone else,' Cathérine continued.

Zazie? Oh, Zazie!

The film *Zazie dans le Métro* always came to mind whenever Cathérine mentioned her white-booted black cat. Arthur was totally crazy about her.

'Of course. I'm here, so no problem at all,' I replied. 'I'll hold the fort.'

It would have been better if I hadn't said that.

'Oh, you poor thing! I hope you won't feel too lonely,' Cathérine replied instantly, watching me again with congenial eyes. 'Now that Arthur's gone, you're all on your own.' Cocking her head, she pursed her lips in sympathy, and I sat straight up in alarm.

'Oh, I'm actually really glad to have some peace and quiet,' I exclaimed reassuringly. 'I need to write.'

I'd said that so often in recent weeks that I almost believed it myself. My words must have sounded convincing, because Cathérine propped her chin in her hand and studied me with interest.

'What's your new book about?' she asked.

I was glad to supply the information now that we had once again left the winding paths of my personal state of mind.

My new novel was about a publisher at a small press, whose energetic engagement managed to just barely keep the company afloat. The publishing industry isn't exactly flourishing these days, after all, and his marriage is in trouble and on the brink of collapse. But one day, lightning strikes. Thanks to a chain reaction of hilarious coincidences, one of his press's novels has been mixed up with a serious literary work of the same title – and it has been unexpectedly nominated for the Prix Goncourt. The novel quickly sells out, and a new edition has to be hurriedly printed, since it has become the season's hottest title. Publishers around the world run up bids in ludicrous auctions to buy the foreign rights. The award jurors find the book 'refreshingly simple' and 'ingeniously framed in colloquial prose'. An immensely wealthy Indian actress wants to create a Bollywood movie based on the novel with herself as the star. Everything gets out of hand, and the individuals responsible for the mix-up are so embarrassed that they refuse to speak up and admit their mistake. At the end of the book, the publisher, sedentary by nature, can no longer contain his delight, and secretly dances around his small garden in the moonlight.

That was also the working title for my new novel, at least as it currently stood: *The Publisher Who Danced in the Moonlight.*

Cathérine had listened attentively. 'Mmm, that all sounds really good. It's sure to be an *amazing* book,' she declared, giving me an encouraging smile.

I smiled back, pleased, and my eyes slid complacently over her water-blue tunic that she had paired with jeans and which matched her eyes quite nicely.

'But I think the title is a little funny.'

'Well, it's supposed to be a humorous novel, Cathérine,' I replied wryly. Good grief! The title was the best part about this stupid book.

When I'd suggested it to him, Jean-Pierre Favre had slapped his legs in delight. 'Marvellous, my dear Julien, it will be absolutely splendid! I'm going to tell the designer right away so he can start on the cover design as soon as possible.'

At the time, we'd both thought I'd dash this book off, lightly and deftly, and it would follow quickly on the heels of my first bestseller.

I took a deep breath and noticed Cathérine's eyes darken.

'I imagine it must be difficult – I mean, to write a funny book like that after everything … everything that's happened,' she stumbled to a halt.

I'm sure she meant well, but she possessed the rare talent of being able to press her delicate fingers into sensitive wounds.

'I hope you know, Julien, that you can call me on my cell any time,' she said. 'I mean, in case you're feeling stir-crazy or you find yourself stuck with your book.'

Like hell I will, I thought as I paid for our meals.

'Sure enough,' I said with a smile.

I actually wrote a lot during that first week. I sat down every morning at my computer, drank black coffee like an idiot, smoked, and hammered out some kind of trivial nonsense. When evening came, I deleted everything I'd written.

Another example of staying busy and not making any progress.

However, I didn't destroy my letters to Hélène.

I told her about my unsuccessful attempts at writing; about Arthur, so glad to be at the seaside with Mamie; about Mamie, whose sister Carole had actually joined them in Honfleur for a few days, after her daughter had offered to take care of her sick father for that time; about Camille, who especially loved wearing Hélène's red dress with the white polka dots and had fallen in love. I wrote about Alexandre, who was very busy getting ready for his spring exhibition, but who had still managed to drop by one evening to make sure I was all right. About Zazie, who I was feeding and who rolled gleefully around on the carpet whenever I opened Cathérine's door.

I started to write to Hélène almost every day – completely unfiltered letters, almost like diary entries. This felt good, and the secret compartment in the gravestone was slowly filling with envelopes. I felt so close to Hélène, as if she were still here, just somewhere else.

And she actually was somewhere, too.

I also wrote about the woman whom Arthur and I had met, and how I had first thought that Arthur was talking with the tree where she'd been sitting. I found myself unconsciously watching for her whenever I went to the Cimetière Montmartre.

Sophie was nowhere to be seen the first time I went back, but that was probably because it was Easter Sunday and she had better things to do than repair angels and gravestones. On the other hand, I discovered a nosegay of forget-me-nots on the grave, which Cathérine had obviously left before her departure. It was raining the next time, and the girl from the cemetery was not around. But my third visit brought the sight of a petite figure in overalls and cap a distance away. She was sitting on top of the roof of a weathered mausoleum and scrubbing at the porous stone with a wire brush.

She waved down from her perch.

'Oh, the author,' she called.

And I said: 'Oh, the sculptor. You're back again?'

'I don't work in the rain.' She climbed down from the roof of the stone structure and wiped dusty hands on her overalls. 'And you? Already back at the cemetery? I thought you wanted to write.'

'I'm trying.'

'And how's my little friend doing?'

'Arthur? Amazingly well, especially since he's away from all of this. He's running down the beach, playing in the waves, collecting shells.

According to my mother, he's happier than he's been in a long time.'

'A walk along the beach is the best therapy,' Sophie asserted, and I laughed because she always seemed to have a platitude at the ready. 'I'd like to go the coast again.' For a moment, her big eyes drifted dreamily across the billowing trees. 'But I have too much to do right now, and we can only work when the weather is good. If the sun is too strong, it's bad for some of the materials, and you can't use the preservatives when it's freezing.' She started to climb back up on the mausoleum.

'Who actually hires you for all this?' I asked quickly. 'The city?'

'Sometimes the city, when the graves that need restoration are old and fall under historic preservation ordinances. But often I'm hired by private clients – descendants of the famous people who are buried here. You'd be surprised.'

We chatted for a few minutes, before she finally climbed back up on the roof of the family crypt, and I left the cemetery and wandered around Montmartre a little. I kept an eye out for Sophie's little bistro but didn't find it. Instead, I walked up Rue des Saules, which led me past green grapevines – remnants of the days when Montmartre had been a hilltop village – and past the Maison Rose, the famous pink house that Picasso used to visit. I finally came to Le Consulat, where years ago Hélène and I had sat outside in the sunshine.

The days were growing brighter and warmer. Even Madame Grenouille forgot that she despised the world, and when we ran into each other in the hallway in front of Cathérine's apartment, she greeted me quite pleasantly, at least for her. She was already aware that her neighbour was on vacation and that I was taking care of her cat. I went downstairs twice a day to look in on her. As soon as she heard me, Zazie would miaow loudly on the other side of the door, and she would enthusiastically rub against my legs when I spooned her food out of the small can and gave her fresh water.

Nonetheless, the high points of those uneventful days were definitely my visits to the cemetery and my conversations with Sophie, which kept my thoughts distracted for a while. I managed well enough as long as they were occupied, even if a flood of despair threatened to engulf me sometimes at night, and sadness would wash over me when I least expected it.

It might be a laughing couple on the street, carefree and holding hands, or a song on the radio – and there it was again, the needle of pain. When I heard about the death of a famous stage actor from the Comédie-Française, the tears welled up in my eyes. I practically never went to the theatre, and I didn't know the individual personally. However, in those days, even the sight of a lonely croissant in my breadbasket was enough to send me off the deep end.

The pretty weather attracted the tourists to the Cimetière Montmartre, and that bothered me as well. At one point, an English school class stood grouped around Heine's grave. The kids were yelling and taking selfie after selfie. I had to stifle an impulse to stride into their midst and cry: '*Shut your fucking mouths! This is a cemetery.*'

On another day, I saw strangers standing arm in arm at Hélène's gravestone, staring pensively at the bronze angel.

'What a lovely face,' the man said.

And before they strolled on to the next grave, I heard the woman say: 'And what a sad poem. I wonder what the story is behind it? She was so young.'

Earlier, before death affected me so deeply, I used to walk around cemeteries the same way. I would read the inscriptions and make up the fate that had played itself out between the dates that demarcated a single life. There rested a child who had never had a chance to fall in love. Here was a man who had followed his wife into the grave only three months later. They were stories that touched me in that moment and made me think, but I left them behind as soon as I stepped back out into the bright flow of life. Today I was restless, like a story with no beginning and no end.

I ran into Sophie once more, three days before Arthur was supposed to return. She was in the process of packing up her tools and leaving, but she must have sensed how forlorn I was feeling that afternoon, because she fussed at me that I came here much too often. She then suggested that we go and have a cup of coffee somewhere.

I gratefully agreed.

'Be honest – why do you come to the cemetery so often, Julien?' she asked, once we were sitting underneath a café awning out on the Place du Tertre.

Her eyes bored into mine, and I felt my cheeks flush. I didn't know how to tell her about the letters in which she herself appeared.

'You're not coming here because of me, are you?' She shook a teasing finger at me.

'I wish I could say that was why ... But I'm always glad to see you, Sophie,' I explained truthfully.

'Doesn't matter.' Her mouth turned up in a mocking smile, as she pointed her spoon at me. 'I have to tell you, Julien, that all this grave-visiting isn't doing you any good. It's lost time that you could make better use of, and it won't bring Hélène back.'

Her brusque manner somehow made everything easier.

'Well . . . I need to make sure everything's in order,' I replied. 'Bring fresh flowers and so on.'

'Yeah, sure.'

She grinned pointedly, and I felt like she'd seen through me. Then with a sudden gesture she pulled off her little cap and shook out her long hair as she turned her face up toward the sun. In amazement, I gazed at the dark torrent that now framed her face.

'Give them while you still can, since on graves, they bloom for no man,' she quoted.

I asked: 'Where did you get all the clever sayings?'

'From my grandmother,' she explained cheekily. 'She was a wise woman – just like me.'

'I'm glad you're sharing some of that wisdom with me, Sophie.'

'That's good. Without me, you'd be lost.'

I would have liked to just sit there, distracted by the buzz of activity around the square and by Sophie's banter, which did me so much good, but then her phone rang.

She laughed and said: 'Should I pick up a baguette?' and: 'Yes . . . me too. See you soon!'

She then turned to me and said: 'I have to go!'

I had absolutely no desire to go back home, so I took the Metro to Saint-Germain and strolled aimlessly through the quarter. I walked down Rue Bonaparte, looked at a couple of picture books at Assouline, and considered purchasing a leather wallet embossed with various letters of the alphabet, then discarded the idea when I saw how much it cost. I finally turned down Rue de Seine and sat down at a table in La Palette to have a small supper.

The waiter had just brought me a glass of red wine when I recognised the man in the gold-rimmed spectacles who was carefully folding his newspaper as he sat in the other corner of the bistro beneath a large oil painting. I tried to hide behind my menu, but it was too late. Jean-Pierre Favre had already seen me.

'Ah, Azoulay, my dear sir!' He hurried over to my table and pulled out a seat for himself. 'What a marvellous surprise! May I join you for a moment, *cher ami*?'

I nodded uncomfortably and tried to smile.

'I'm so glad to see that you leave your apartment occasionally,' he said with a wink. 'I was worried you might have barricaded yourself inside.'

We hadn't been in communication since the silent note that had been pushed back and forth underneath my door a few weeks ago.

'How are you doing? I was just thinking about you yesterday, and I was going to call you. We have the perfect cover for the novel lined up.'

I feigned enthusiasm. After all, the novel was my novel.

'All we need now is the finished manuscript,' the publisher joked, pushing up his round glasses, which had a tendency to slip down his narrow nose every few minutes. 'I hope the writing's going well?'

'Oh yes, very well,' I lied valiantly, taking a gulp of my wine. 'I have almost fifty new pages. Just have to put your mind to it.'

'That's what I said!' Favre cried, swaying backward and forward in his delight. 'You just have to *start*. Write the first sentence. That's the secret.'

He waved at the waiter and ordered himself a glass of red wine. He clearly had no intention of leaving any time soon, now that he had managed to get his hands on his author.

He seemed to be calculating numbers and dates, at the end of which he smiled contentedly. 'That means we'll be able to release the book next spring. Bravo, Azoulay! I'm so proud of you! That is quite *formidable.*' His eyes beamed at me. 'You've made it over the hump, haven't you? I always knew you'd be able to do that in the end.'

I silently sipped my wine and nodded.

'*The Publisher Who Danced in the Moonlight* – that will be a winner! I can feel it in my bones, and that means money, my friend.' He gave a little clap.

His excitement rendered me speechless.

How in the world could I destroy his hopes?

I desperately needed a cigarette, but I would have to go outside to do that. I drained my glass in a single draught and gazed at him resolutely.

'However . . . ' I started.

'However?' Jean-Pierre Favre echoed, his eyes flickering with a little concern.

I ran my fingers through my hair. 'I'm not completely convinced that what I'm writing is any good,' I explained contritely, deciding not to share the inglorious fact that in reality I hadn't written anything.

'Ah, the butterflies are all part of it,' Favre asserted, dismissing my assessment with a wave of his hand. 'That's what I like so much about you, Azoulay. Your self-doubt makes you more critical of your own work. Your text ends up better because of it.'

'That might be, but I sometimes think that what I'm writing is utter rubbish, and then I wonder who in the world will actually want to read it,' I sighed. 'At this rate, there'll end up being only one reader of my books. Me!'

'Oh, hogwash! Stop talking such nonsense, Azoulay! Shall I tell you something?' He shot a triumphant look at me. 'You *can't* write rubbish. That's what I say, as your publisher.'

With these promising words, Jean-Pierre Favre stood up and patted me on the shoulder. 'Don't worry, Julien. You'll do it. The book is practically done, right? And you'll find the last sentences as well.'

I watched him pay his bill and stride jauntily out of La Palette. I wasn't so sure. I would have to tell him the truth eventually. How long should I keep him in the dark?

I jabbed despondently at my quiche Lorraine, unaware that something would happen next day that should give months of inspiration to a proper writer.

9

Could you please hold me?

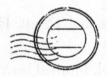

Everything was perfectly normal the next morning. I got up, drank my coffee at the small, round table at the balcony window, and skimmed the newspaper. The same as always, except that the phone would not stop ringing.

All right, that might exaggerate – but for me, the influx of phone calls on that Saturday morning was quite high.

The first was from Maman, who wanted to know if it would be all right if they stayed a few more days in Honfleur. It was so pretty up there, and the weekend trains were always so full. Without asking, she then handed me over to Aunt Carole, who raved at length about a fish soup containing tiny, live baby fish which she had eaten the evening before in a harbour tavern. At the words 'baby fish', my stomach lurched. It wasn't even ten o'clock yet, and since I'm not exactly a child of the Atlantic, the thought of living proteins from the ocean didn't possess even the slightest appeal at this time of day. The most protein I can stomach at breakfast is two fried eggs.

Arthur was the last one on the phone. He giggled secretively and told me that he was going to bring something back for me.

'You will be as happy as . . . an elephant,' he declared proudly.

I have no idea how happy elephants are, but I admired my child's fancies.

'I'll be as happy as an elephant when you get back home,' I said with a smile.

'Can't wait, Papa! Hugs and kisses!' He blew two kisses before hanging up.

Feeling a little emotional, I turned back to *Le Figaro*, but then the phone rang again. This time it was Alexandre, who wanted to make sure that I was still coming to his spring exhibition.

'Everything still on for tonight?' he asked.

'Absolutely,' I replied.

'Gabrielle is bringing her sister along. She's single, too.'

I groaned. 'Alexandre, stop trying to set me up.'

'Her name's Elsa, and she also writes. Just like you,' he added extraneously. 'You'll have something to talk about. Gabrielle has told her all about you. She's looking forward to meeting you.'

I had no desire to meet this Elsa.

The reality is that no writer really wants to spend time with other writers. That is why the author evenings some publishers organise end up being so tedious.

'What does she write?' I asked sceptically.

'Poetry, I think.' My friend laughed cluelessly.

'And her name is really *Elsa*?'

'Yes, no, don't know . . . Who cares? Elsa or Else. It might be her pen name. She always signs her autographs as Elsa L. or something like that.'

I instantly envisioned an exalted creature in palazzo pants and a garish scarf knotted around her forehead, who frequented literary circles and who believed herself to be an Egyptian prince, just like her role model.

All the same, the poet was Gabrielle's sister, and she was unique too.

I could already imagine standing beside Elsa L. in L'éspace des rêveurs.

'*With whom do I have the honour of speaking?*'

'*Prince Yussuf.*'

'*You're Elsa L.?*'

'*That's what they used to call me, but now I am Prince Yussuf. I would like to welcome you to Thebes, the city where I am prince.*'

It would be grand.

'And does she also look like Else Lasker-Schüler?' I asked.

'Like *who*?'

'Forget it.'

'Julien, what are you blabbering about? She looks fantastic, otherwise I wouldn't have invited her. Besides, maybe she'll write a few new verses for my poetry chains. So, I'll see you tonight, my friend. Don't you dare bail on me!'

The third call was from Cathérine. She was back from Le Havre and wanted to thank me for taking such good care of her cat.

'I'm out running a few errands,' she said, obviously in a breezy mood. 'May I drop by later to get the key?'

'Sure,' I said.

*

The hours ticked by, as my anticipation for the approaching evening dwindled. I pottered around the apartment, stretched out on the couch after lunch to read, and postponed the moment I had to leave the house to meet Prince Yussuf.

Alexandre's invitation had mentioned seven o'clock as the starting time, but there was no reason to be one of the first guests. Around 6.45 I finally tossed my book in the corner, and went with a sigh into the bathroom to take a shower. I was just towelling off my hair when another bell rang – this time the doorbell. I wrapped the towel around my waist and padded over to the door, my feet still damp. One look through the peephole revealed that it was Cathérine who was standing at the door. She waited a moment before ringing again.

The key, she wanted the key back! Where had I put it? I rummaged through the bowl sitting on the chest in the hallway, but it wasn't there.

I opened the door a crack and saw that she was holding a wine bottle.

'*Salut*, Cathérine,' I called. 'I'm just getting out of the shower. I'll bring the key down in a few minutes, all right?'

Without waiting for her answer, I shut the door.

When I rang her doorbell about fifteen minutes later, dressed in shirt, trousers and jacket, Cathérine pulled the door open all the way, as if she'd been waiting on me. Behind her, Zazie threw herself on the floor and rolled around, purring.

'Ah, Julien, there you are!' Cathérine smiled brightly, and something was different about her.

Her skin was tanned, and her slender arms extended from a blue-striped spring dress. Her eyes glittered, as small turquoise-coloured teardrops dangled from her pretty ears, which I was noticing for the first time because her hair was pulled back.

'Come in!'

The delicate scent of lily-of-the-valley wafted toward me.

I shook my head and held out her key.

'I don't have time. I've been invited to an exhibition.'

'That's all right! Just come in for a minute,' she insisted, leading the way into the living room.

I followed her hesitantly. As I walked past the kitchen, I caught the smell of thyme and spicy meat.

The table was set, and an opened bottle of wine and two glasses stood on the sideboard.

Before I could protest, Cathérine poured some wine into the glasses and handed me one of them.

'Thank you so very much for taking such good care of Zazie,' she said effusively. 'Try it. It's good. I brought you a bottle as a little thank you.'

'But that isn't necessary, Cathérine,' I protested. 'I live right here.'

'Yes, it's nice that you live right here. That makes me really happy sometimes.'

I pointed at the table. 'Are you expecting company?'

'Yes and no,' she replied. 'My friend just cancelled on me. Stomach bug.'

'Oh no, how awful.'

'Yes.' She nodded, and then gave me another strange smile. 'And now, here I am with my Tuscan-style lasagne ... I don't really want to have Madame Grenouille over to eat ... I'm sure she'd have the time, but ...'

Her eyes sparkled, and I sensed where all this was going.

'Sorry about your evening,' I said, setting down my glass. 'But I really have to go now. I'm late as it is.'

I glanced at the clock. It was already seven-thirty.

I don't know how she did it, but suddenly she was standing right in front of me in her blue dress, blocking my path and gazing at me with her pleading Julie Delpy eyes.

'Please stay a little while, Julien! You could eat a little lasagne with me and still make it to your exhibition.' Her cheeks were flushed.

I shook my head in confusion: 'But Cathérine, I . . .'

'Please!' She stared at me unwaveringly. 'Didn't you know today's my birthday?'

No, I hadn't. Hélène had always taken care of the birthdays.

'Oh, dear,' I said.

What else could I have done? I stayed with her, since after all I wasn't an utter monster. You couldn't just up and leave a young woman who had not only lost her best friend, but whose plans had come apart on her thirty-second birthday.

Besides, Cathérine's homemade lasagne was bound to be quite a bit better than whatever appetisers Alexandre had arranged for his exhibition. The stunning Elsa L. was going to have to find someone else to talk to.

And just like that, I opened the door to fate.

That evening, my wife's friend experienced her shining hour. She was so grateful that I stayed with her that she mobilised all of her wit and charm to keep me entertained. I must admit that it didn't take too long for me to feel quite at ease, due to the delicious meal, the good, slightly heavy red wine with which Cathérine kept refilling my glass, the subdued music, and the candles she had lit.

'I'm really sorry I forgot your birthday,' I said at some point.

After opening the second bottle of wine, we had relocated to her beige linen sofas, which faced each other across a glass coffee table. I had realised long before this point that I wouldn't be going to Alexandre's exhibition, although we had discussed it early on. While we were eating, I had even suggested that Cathérine come along with me, if she didn't want to stay home alone.

A floor lamp was burning in the corner, suffusing the room with a soft glow. The table was still cluttered with the uncleared dishes and the candles that were gradually burning low.

My head spun a little from the wine. Zazie had curled into a ball on the cushion next to me, and I felt almost as sluggish as a full cat.

Cathérine was scraping the last bit of tiramisu from her bowl and staring absently at the candles flickering on the dining table.

'These birthdays,' she said, setting her bowl down next to mine. 'For my thirtieth birthday two years ago, we celebrated together at the Vieux Colombier. Remember?'

I nodded pensively. I still recalled in detail the small, cosy brasserie close to the Church of Saint-Sulpice and the countless glasses of red wine we had drunk together to Cathérine's good health. Hélène, Cathérine and I had been the last ones to leave, swaying and laughing. We didn't have far to walk.

Two Aprils ago, the world had still been in order. But by June of that year, the first cracks in the surface were beginning to show, and the chasm was gaping beneath them.

I sighed, overwhelmed by a feeling of deep melancholy.

Cathérine also sighed, and as if she had read my thoughts, she said sadly: 'Hélène was still here.' She fell silent for a moment. 'She never forgot a birthday,' she resumed. 'She always wrote me the best birthday cards ... I ... I still have all of them, and sometimes ...'

She broke off abruptly and covered her mouth with her hand, her eyes shimmering. 'I miss her so much,' she whispered. 'I don't know what to do with all of it.' She gazed at me unhappily. 'Oh, Julien!'

'Oh, Cathérine,' I murmured. 'I miss her too.'

'What are we supposed to do? What are we supposed to do now?'

She uttered the question twice, and each time, it felt like a dagger thrust into my heart. Because the answer would always be the same.

Nothing. There was nothing we could do.

I stood up heavily from the couch.

'I think it's time for us to say goodnight, Cathérine,' I said gently. 'Thank you again for the meal.'

She got to her feet, swaying slightly. 'Thank you for staying with me, Julien.'

I walked over to the door, and she followed me into the narrow entryway.

'Well, sweet dreams,' I said helplessly.

She nodded and attempted a smile. 'Thanks, you too.'

I turned the knob and looked back one more time.

I shouldn't have done that.

Cathérine's face had crumpled into misery. She was wringing her hands, and tears were rolling down her cheeks. She let out a hiccuping sob, and her despair dissolved the floor beneath my feet.

'Oh no, Cathérine ... Cathérine, no, please don't,' I begged, releasing the doorknob.

'Could you please hold me?'

She was sobbing bitterly, and I was now crying too, so I wrapped my arms around her. We stood there for a long time in the narrow, dark hallway, clinging to each other like we were drowning. Until the despair suddenly turned into an overpowering longing. For comfort, for closeness, for human touch.

Enveloped by her lily-of-the-valley perfume, our hands began to move. I found Cathérine's mouth, soft and swollen from crying. She tasted like tiramisu. And for the first time after all the sad weeks and months, I was once again holding a woman in my arms – a warm, affectionate, living creature who drew me to herself. I lurched after her into the bedroom as after a promise.

We were both emotionally battered, and we had both drunk far too much wine. And I knew that we were on the brink of a precipice. This was exactly the kind of thing that happened in the middle of the night when you were standing at a precipice. However, that didn't stop me from slipping Cathérine's dress off her shoulders. I heard her quiet sigh, and buried my face between her breasts.

10

Lost certainties

Early in the morning, I crept out of Cathérine's apartment like a thief in the night.

She'd still been asleep when I woke up. I was momentarily confused when I opened my eyes in a strange bedroom, and then I was overcome by a feeling of great unease. I looked at Cathérine's quietly slumbering face with its smears of mascara, and gently moved her bare arm from where it was resting heavily on my shoulder.

What had I done? What had we done?

My skull was pounding as I slipped out of the bed, striving to be quiet in the dim light as I gathered up my clothes from the floor. Shoes in hand, I tiptoed to the door. It felt like a scene from a farce.

From her cat basket, Zazie's shimmering eyes followed me, and she mewed softly. Fortunately, she was the only witness of that night-time incident, which had at least occurred in Cathérine's apartment and not in mine. What would have happened if Cathérine had brought her wine and her loneliness up to me, and Arthur had been back and had stood at the bed, wide-eyed, and then asked in his bright child's voice: 'Is Cathérine now sleeping in Maman's bed?' I felt sick at the very thought.

I quietly pulled the apartment door shut behind me and was about to put my shoes on when the door across the hallway opened.

In shock, I spun around. It was only a few minutes after six. Who in the world was up at this hour on a Sunday?

Madame Grenouille assessed the situation in a single glance. To be honest, that wasn't particularly difficult. My guilty conscience was written all over my face. The old woman inhaled indignantly and shook her head disapprovingly before she gasped:

'Un-be-liev-a-ble!'

I hurried past her and up the stairs in my socks, her malicious eyes in my back. I could imagine her airing her outrage in the small bou-langerie on Rue Jacob, where I always bought my baguettes.

'Just imagine it, Madame. His poor wife only in the ground for six months, and he's already consoling himself with her friend. All I can say is, isn't that just like a man?!'

And then she would take her bag of croissants and say 'Unbelievable!' again. The friendly clerk, the one who always had a few kind words for me in the morning – me, the unfortunate widower – would nod and then just stare at me next time, as if I were a callous monster.

And it was *unbelievable*, I agreed, as I measured much too much ground coffee into the silver espresso maker. I needed to clear my mind.

Cathérine of all people!

The scent of lily-of-the-valley still seemed to cling to me.

I took a shower while the coffee bubbled over the gas flame. As the water splashed down my back, I reviewed what had happened the previous evening.

It had been both bewildering and wonderful to hold Cathérine in my arms, to kiss her and to feel alive again. I couldn't dispute that. There hadn't been a single second in which I'd felt that uncomfortable feeling that immediately arises whenever two bodies aren't in harmony. Her loyalty, her warmth, I had taken pleasure in all that – intoxicated by the wine and by my longing to fill the horrible void that was threatening to consume me. However, when I woke up and saw her next to me, I immediately felt that I'd made a huge mistake. I'd let myself get carried away, and on top of that, I felt as if I had betrayed Hélène twice over.

My wife's friend – that had been so banal, so shameful, maybe a little too easy. And I already suspected that everything would now become terribly complicated.

Cathérine was like a sister to me – or better said, a distant cousin – but would she also see it that way?

I turned off the water and wrapped a towel around me.

My cellphone was sitting on the kitchen table, and it was buzzing. It was Cathérine, who had obviously noticed my disappearance already.

I didn't answer, but turned on the radio instead.

A woman was singing a sad song, and when she reached the words *Don't you wish that we could forget that kiss, and see this for what it is, that we're not in love,* I cut the radio back off.

The coffee was so strong that after the first sip, I couldn't keep my hand steady. I didn't mind. I pulled out an old package of cookies from the cabinet and dunked them in the black brew.

My phone buzzed again. This time it was Alexandre, and I answered.

'Where were you yesterday? I can't believe you blew me off,' he snarled. 'I always knew you weren't going to come.'

'It's not what you think,' I said.

'*You can't be serious*! What kind of effing shit was that?!' Alexandre hollered when I told him about the night with Cathérine.

Although he makes delicate goldwork, my friend can sometimes swear like a harbour worker from Marseille. And yet even the worst profanity somehow comes out of his mouth sounding civilised. 'You hooked up with *Cathérine?*'

'That might not be the right phrase in this instance,' I quickly interjected. 'We were both really sentimental last night – and it just kind of happened.'

'And now?'

'Ask me something easier.'

'You should've come to my exhibition.'

I didn't reply and took a sip from my lethal concoction. Hindsight is always twenty-twenty.

'Was it at least nice?'

'At the time it was, otherwise I wouldn't have stayed the night. She looked so pretty, and I felt so sorry for her and for me, too ... somehow ...' I trailed off.

Alexandre seemed to consider something for a moment.

'Want to know what I think?' he asked finally.

'No.'

'Two unhappy people can't comfort each other.'

'Thanks for the tip,' I said, rubbing my temples.

'At least if they're unhappy about the same person. There's no way that can work.'

I didn't contradict him. It seemed to work just fine in the novels written by certain authors.

'I just feel wretched,' I said.

'I'm not surprised. What has Cathérine said?'

'No idea. She called a few minutes ago, but I didn't answer.'

'Man, oh man!' Alexandre sighed, and I sighed, too. 'Boy, you've screwed things up royally. Everyone knows to keep their fingers off their wives' friends. That's the fastest way to cause all sorts of trouble.'

'Really, Einstein? I thought that was only true when the wife was still alive.'

'That's true, too.' He laughed guardedly. 'Don't worry, Julien, it'll all blow over. It was actually a very human thing, wasn't it? Didn't someone once say that under certain circumstances we could fall in love with anyone?'

'But I don't *love* her,' I cried. What was he talking about? 'It was just a stupid cocktail of various factors that made it happen.'

'I know, Julien, I know,' he said soothingly. 'And believe me, it could have been worse.'

'I doubt it.'

'It's true! At the party, Elsa L. turned out to be a man-eater. Just be happy you didn't fall into her clutches. You wouldn't have been able to get rid of her as quickly as your pretty neighbour.'

'What do mean *get rid of*? That's not what I'm trying to do. I don't want to get rid of Cathérine.' For some reason, I felt a need to defend her. 'I don't have anything against her. I just need to make it clear to her that last night was a one-time thing.'

'If it's that easy, then *talk* to her.'

Alexandre hung up, and I stared at my phone, hoping that Cathérine would call one more time during the course of the day. But my wife's friend didn't do that, nor did she leave a message.

Her silence bothered me. For the next two days, it seemed as if Cathérine had dropped off the face of the planet. I didn't risk calling her, since it was best not to discuss such things on the phone. One evening, I timidly rang her doorbell, but she didn't answer. I was actually relieved to go back upstairs. I'd managed to convince myself that perhaps the whole thing had been just as unpleasant for her as it had been for me. Or did she just happen to be out, but was constantly checking her phone to see if I had called? I, her betrayer.

Whatever the case, the radio silence made me nervous.

On the day of Arthur's return, I ran into her by accident that morning in my *traîteur* on Rue de Buci, where I was picking up a few peaches, some cheese, puff pastry tarts, and little meatballs in marinara sauce, one of Arthur's favourites.

We stood there with our bags, looking at each other in embarrassment.

'*Salut*, Julien.'

'*Salut*, Cathérine.'

'How are you doing?'

'Oh, good ... good. And you?'

'Yes ... also good.'

We didn't say anything for a moment, then we both said simultaneously: 'I ...'

'Yes?' She looked at me in suspense.

'No, you first.'

'No, no, you ...'

It couldn't keep going this way. Nor could we keep standing between the French bean salad with bacon and the stuffed crabs in their pink shell-shaped containers.

'Would you like to have a cup of coffee somewhere?'

She nodded.

It wasn't easy. Our conversation got off to a bumpy start. We were both self-conscious, and neither of us wanted to offend the other.

'I'm so sorry, Julien. I don't understand how that could have happened,' Cathérine said, and looked ashamed. 'But I . . .'

She shook her head and seemed to be really angry that, in her empathy for me and my situation, she had managed to miss her mark so widely.

'And then you just tiptoed away the next morning, and I didn't know, I didn't know . . .' Her eyes held a plea.

'That wasn't right of me,' I said quickly. 'But I was so bewildered that morning, and now it feels like I betrayed Hélène. I feel awful.'

'No, Julien, don't beat yourself up over this.' Cathérine leaned forward and patted my arm briefly. 'It was . . . Uh, I'm not sure either. It was just the situation, right?' Her eyes were doubtful. 'Do you think Hélène would be upset with us?'

Fingers in the wounds, I thought. *Fingers in the wounds*.

I shook my head helplessly and didn't answer the question.

There was no *us*, only the sad unavoidable companionship on Rue Jacob.

'Oh, Julien! We're just both kind of unhinged these days,' Cathérine declared. 'Otherwise, it wouldn't have happened.' Her blue eyes watched me steadfastly. 'But it has to get better sooner or later.'

I nodded. 'Yes, sooner or later, exactly.'

We sipped our coffee and stayed sitting, both at a loss.

'Know what, Cathérine?' I finally said. 'I think a good relationship is based on hope, not on mutual pity.'

She nodded. 'But . . . We can still be friends, right, Julien?' she asked uncertainly.

'Of course, Cathérine! What are you thinking? Of course we'll still be friends!'

I really meant it, too. In that moment, I was so relieved we'd finally been able to talk things out. However, there was one thing I wasn't thinking about: Cathérine and I had never been friends. She was my wife's friend. We didn't have any common history. And whenever I saw her during the following weeks – when we ran into each other in the entry area, or I picked up Arthur from her apartment – I always had the feeling that the ground beneath me was slightly unsteady.

Hélène, my beloved Hélène,

The last few days have flown by. I had planned to go to Alexandre's party on Saturday evening – I wrote you about it, as you might recall – but all of a sudden, Cathérine was standing at my door with a bottle of wine. It was her birthday, and she didn't want to celebrate alone. A friend of hers had apparently cancelled on her at the last minute, and as you might suspect already, I ended up unexpectedly enjoying her marvellous lasagne.

Cathérine was so happy I stayed with her, and it wasn't any great sacrifice from my end. I must confess I wasn't all that thrilled about going to the exhibition anyway. Alexandre means well, but I'm not ready yet to socialise with people I don't know. I quickly feel quite lost in such situations. It's nothing like it was earlier, when you and I would go places together. Even if we didn't spend the entire time at each other's side, our eyes would meet over and over again across the room and over people's heads. With you at my side, dearest, I would have felt just fine at any kind of party. It feels strange to go everywhere on my own now. And mainly, to leave all alone. I walk down the street and feel somehow incomplete, alone with my thoughts. No post-event discussions, nothing amusing to recall. This is taking some time to get used to.

So instead of the spring exhibition at L'espace des rêveurs, I spent a cosy evening in with Cathérine. We talked a lot about you, Hélène, and about the old times. It was really nice, but when we thought back to Cathérine's thirtieth birthday, we both started feeling really sad.

'I miss her so much. I don't know what to do with it all,' Cathérine said.

Her words went straight through my heart. How quickly all of our lives have changed – in just two years. You are missed all over, Hélène. Oh, how you are missed!

Cathérine has Zazie, and I have Arthur, but nothing, nothing, can fill this terrible void you have left behind. We toasted you, my darling, and thought about you, and how differently the evening would have gone if you'd been there!

Arthur returned from Honfleur the day before yesterday. He came stomping up the stairs, holding Mamie's hand and sporting a new tan. He jumped into my arms. I know it's impossible, but it seems as if he grew a little taller while he was gone. I can't begin to tell you how happy I am that he's back. It was so very quiet without our boy here. Now the apartment is filled with life again. And with toys. You wouldn't believe how quickly he pulled out his things and scattered them all over. Someday I'm going to slip on one of his damned Playmobil figures and break my leg.

Just imagine: he brought a gift for me, and was so extremely proud of it. He had actually found a starfish on the beach. It's supposed to bring me luck, he told me. We spent hours figuring out the best place for the starfish. Arthur can be a very conscientious little boy sometimes. He vacillated for a long time between my nightstand and my desk, but now the starfish is sitting in all of its beauty on the desk in front of your picture. So you can see it, too, Arthur explained.

It had been ages since Maman and Aunt Carole had spent so much time together without arguing. Everything must have been quite peaceful. The days at the beach also did my aunt a world of good, and the sisters were able to talk about all sorts of things. It isn't always a walk in the park for Carole, having to deal with Paul and his illness. He can't be left alone for even a moment. But Camille seems to have done all right with him.

And now for some good news! Camille is pregnant – by that nice man she met a few months ago. Talk about fast! But the two of them must be incredibly happy. The prospect of having a baby can bring such a rush of hope. Camille even told her father about it.

'Papa, I'm going to have a baby,' she said.

And old Paul supposedly smiled at her blissfully and asked: 'Is it mine?'

You see how funny it actually would be if everything weren't so sad.

Maman told me that you have to trust in life itself, and that, in the end, everything will make sense. But when it comes to your death, my darling, I still can't see any sense at all.

I plan to go to the cemetery tomorrow and take you my letter. I can hardly believe this is already the twentieth I've written to you. Yes, sweetheart, I'm catching up, and it's ended up being easier than I'd thought it would be. My voice, your silence. I wonder if you are seeing any of what is happening down here.

Sometimes I think yes, sometimes no. And sometimes I just wish that I could receive an answer from you. Just once, that's all.

But that will never happen, and so I'll just remain, until we can be together again,

Your deeply saddened

Julien

Dearest Hélène,

Arthur discovered our little secret yesterday. This is what happened.

I had wanted to go to the cemetery in the morning, but then the nursery school called. Arthur had a stomach ache and wanted to go home, so could I please come and pick him up? When I got to the nursery, he was already feeling better. The teacher winked at me and said it was probably more mental than physical. He obviously wanted to be with me. Perhaps he was having a hard time adjusting from his holiday back to life at home. So I decided to take him along to the cemetery.

We had hardly walked inside the gates and started down the path to your grave, when he caught sight of the conservator I already told you about. She was working on a weathered angel sculpture, and Arthur insisted on staying with her to see how she was going to reattach a broken wing.

'May I watch for a few minutes, Papa?' he wheedled, and since Sophie didn't mind, I left him there and went on to your grave.

I studied the countenance of the angel who gazes out, both day and night, and her face suddenly seemed more forbidding, her mouth more stern.

I had just placed the letter in the compartment, when Arthur popped up, watching me.

'What are you doing, Papa?' he asked brightly.

'Oh . . . well, I sometimes write letters to Maman,' I confessed guiltily. 'And to keep the letters from spoiling, I put them in this little mailbox.'

'Cool,' he said. That's what all the kids in his class say – 'Cool.' The letters didn't seem to bother him at all. 'She'll like getting them. It's probably boring up in heaven sometimes,' was his commentary. 'Too bad I can't write yet. When I can, I'll write her some letters too.'

I shut the little door and said: 'But this is a secret, Arthur. Don't tell anyone about it, all right? Nobody. Otherwise . . . otherwise, the letters won't be picked up.'

He nodded solemnly. 'I won't tell, Papa,' he promised earnestly. 'I know what a secret is. I'm not a baby any more.'

He took my hand, and as we walked back along the path we saw Sophie sitting on a bench in the sunshine, eating her lunch. She had brought along several tartines and a small bottle of beer and she offered to share her sandwiches with us. Arthur talked a blue streak, describing everything that had happened on his trip to the beach. I was far off, lost in my own thoughts.

Oh, Hélène! There's something weighing heavily on me. I also *have a secret, and it's not a nice one. Maybe you already know about it, if you are actually still here, somewhere, looking down on us.*

I wasn't completely honest with you, my dearest! That evening with Cathérine, that birthday evening I wrote about ... it ended very differently.

It's true that we were both very sad, and it's also true that we were both thinking a lot about you. But then, I don't know how, we suddenly fell sobbing into each other's arms. One thing led to another, and we ended up spending the night together.

I'm so horribly ashamed, Hélène. I don't love Cathérine, not even a little. We were both so unhappy that evening, and we clung to each other for support. It was wrong. It was a mistake. But I miss you so much all the time, and you are gone for ever. That's hard to cope with. Oh, if only I could have you back! If only my letters could make you come back to life, I would write a thousand letters!

And now I am sitting here with my guilty conscience, hoping that you can forgive me.

'Would Hélène be upset with us?' Cathérine asked when we were talking through everything.

I didn't have an answer for that. It feels as if I betrayed my darling Hélène. That is what you are for me, my darling.

Can you forgive us? Can you forgive me?

If only you could send an answer, you ever-silent angel send a sign to show me that everything is all right. I would give anything for that!

I love you, my angel. I will always love you.

Forgive me!

Julien

11

Good spirits

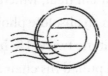

It would be May before I made it back to the Cimetière Montmartre.

Maybe it was all the excitement with Cathérine, maybe the cold wind that was blowing across the Pont des Arts after I'd spent an evening with Alexandre close to Beaubourg. Or maybe it was Maxime, Arthur's little friend from nursery school, who came over one afternoon and coughed all over me as we played Rabbit and Hedgehog. Whatever the case, I came down with the flu, and was laid flat out. My head roared, and my arms and legs ached. I couldn't recall the last time I'd even run a low fever in the past few years. What I ran now made up for that. I dragged myself from bed to bathroom and then back to bed, helped Arthur get dressed in the morning, stuck a film in for him in the afternoon, and that was about it.

During this time, I learned to value the good-hearted people who seemed to pop up everywhere to help me. Maman advised me to not go to the doctor – 'They can't do anything for the flu anyway, and all you'll do is catch more germs in the waiting room' – and came over every day to cook for us. I even managed to gain some weight during the fourteen days of my illness, which was anything but typical. Élodie – the mother of Arthur's coughing playmate, who was no longer coughing by this point – rang our bell every morning and took the children to nursery school. From the onset, Cathérine volunteered to pick Arthur up in the afternoons and to play with him on the days she could. She also frequently brought me, the patient, a small treat, which I accepted gratefully.

Even Alexandre, who has an absolute phobia when it comes to bacteria and viruses, came to visit me twice. He held a handkerchief in front of his mouth and nose, and pulled his chair as far away as possible from the sofa I was stretched on.

I slept a lot during this time. My body waged its battle against the virus, and so I dozed on, aided by half-closed curtains and some effective pain tablets, which put me in a peaceful frame of mind.

One time, I dreamed about Hélène. She appeared before me, smiling, in a white robe with a crown of daisies in her hair. Was this the current fashion up in heaven? She kissed me softly on the lips and said:

'I wanted to look in on you, Julien. Are you doing all right?'

'Now I am,' I sighed, relieved that she was back. 'Please don't leave again, Hélène. I need you so much.'

'But Julien, *mon drôle de mari,*' she replied with a gentle laugh. 'I'm always with you. Didn't you know that?'

She sat on the edge of the bed and tenderly brushed the sweaty hair back from my forehead. I grasped her hand, which was so long and slender. *I simply won't let it go,* I thought. *I won't ever let this hand go.* I blissfully closed my eyes. Everything was good again. Hélène was with me, and I clutched her hand tightly . . .

And when I woke up, I found myself still holding one of the bedposts. I stared at the wood for an age, in disbelief.

One afternoon – I was well on my way to recovery at this point – Cathérine brought Arthur back home and lingered a little indecisively in the living room. She obviously had something on her mind. We could hear Arthur singing in his room, where he was sitting at his little table and colouring one picture after another, his newest favourite activity. Cathérine raised a finger to her lips and quietly shut the living-room door.

I pulled myself up against my pillow. What was she doing?

'Julien, we need to talk,' she explained quietly, as she sat down on one of the armchairs across from the couch. 'It's about Arthur.'

'What about Arthur?' I asked in alarm. 'What's wrong? Is he being bullied at nursery school?'

The newspapers were constantly running articles about children being marginalised and made fun of by their classmates.

'No, no, that's not it,' she began hesitantly.

'Then what is it?'

Her cheeks suddenly flushed bright red. 'Today Arthur asked me if I was going to be his new Maman.'

'*What*?! Where'd he get that idea?' I cried suspiciously.

'I asked him, and he told me that he ran into Madame Grenouille this morning on the stairs. She said something about him being an unfortunate little boy whose heartless Papa had already forgotten his dead Maman, since he had a new girlfriend, that teacher whose apartment he was visiting in the evenings. "You'll soon be getting a stepmother, you poor, poor boy!" she added.'

'That old witch!' I could feel the adrenalin shooting through my veins. 'I could wring her neck!'

'Bad idea, otherwise Arthur will also be without a Papa. But how did she know?'

I sighed and leaned back into the pillows.

'Well,' I said shamefacedly. 'She saw me that time as I ... you know ... left your apartment early in the morning. She was just suddenly there at her door, giving me the evil eye.'

Cathérine gave a brief chuckle before turning serious again.

'You need to talk to Arthur and explain it to him somehow,' she declared. 'I told him that we're just good friends.' Her gaze was doubtful, and her eyes held something I couldn't identify. 'That was the right thing to do, don't you think?'

'Definitely,' I confirmed. 'You handled it just fine, Cathérine. I'll talk to Arthur later.'

'Good.' She stood up, picked up her briefcase, and opened the living-room door again. 'See you tomorrow.'

She raised her hand in farewell, and I waved back.

'And ... Cathérine?'

'Yes?'

'Thank you. For everything.'

That evening, I watched *Robin Hood* with Arthur again. We sat together on the sofa – he in his pyjamas with the brown teddy bears, me in my striped ones. A large bowl of crisps was sitting between us, which we were sharing companionably, and Arthur was huddled under a blanket.

He crowed with delight every time Robin Hood played a trick on the Sheriff of Nottingham. At the end of the thrilling adventures, when sly Robin pulled Maid Marian into his arms and little hearts danced around the two foxes, Arthur sighed happily.

He then looked over at me.

'Papa . . . know what?' He giggled a little.

'No, but I bet you're about to tell me, little one.' I pulled him into a hug, and he rested his head against my shoulder.

'I have a girlfriend, too,' he explained dreamily.

'What?!' I looked at him, astonished. 'Isn't it a little early for that, Arthur? You're only four.'

'No, Papa,' he assured me. 'Maxime also has a girlfriend.'

'Aha!' I said. What did I know? I was just the father.

'But mine is prettier,' Arthur continued. 'She has red curls like Maman.' He sighed contentedly and stretched out his legs. 'Giulietta is the prettiest girl in the Smurf group. Her Maman is Italian,' he declared proudly.

'That's . . . that's great.' I was a little confused. 'And – I mean . . . what happens when you have a girlfriend?' I asked cautiously.

'Oh, Papa,' he said. 'It's really easy.' He picked up a handful of chips and chewed contentedly. 'You pick one out, ask her: "Do you want to go with me?" and she says: "Yes."' He shot me a quick look. 'If she heard you, that is . . . ' he explained, as I bit back a smile. 'And then you give each other a kiss, and then you're together.'

'Oh . . . wow!' I said relieved. 'And she . . . Giulietta . . . *heard* you right away when you asked?'

'Yes.' He smiled, snuggling closer against me. 'We sit next to each other at lunchtime and save places for each other. She thinks I'm cool, you know.'

'Well, you are definitely a cool dude,' I agreed, tousling his dark curls and making the snap decision to grab the bull by the horns.

'Know what? I need to tell you something, too, Arthur.'

He watched me with big eyes. 'About Cathérine?' he asked.

I nodded. 'Yes. Cathérine and I, we're friends,' I began. 'But . . . but we're not *going* together. Understand?'

He nodded sceptically. 'But Madame Grenouille said—'

'Madame Grenouille is a silly old woman who likes to say bad things about people and other stupid stuff,' I interrupted him. 'She saw me walk out of Cathérine's apartment one morning while you were still in Honfleur with Mamie. I was just comforting Cathérine, because it was her birthday and she was all alone. I stayed with her that night so she wouldn't be so sad.' At least, it wasn't a complete lie. 'Does that make sense?'

Arthur seemed to accept this. 'It does, Papa. Cathérine also told me that you're just good friends.'

'Exactly.' I nodded in relief.

'But you know what else?'

'No, what?'

'It's all right if you want her to be my new Maman. She's so nice, not like the wicked stepmother in *Cinderella*.' He gave a big yawn.

'You're right about that,' I agreed. 'But still – Cathérine and I are just friends. And it'll stay that way.'

He nodded sleepily, and I took him to bed.

That night I dreamed about a small red-haired girl name Giulietta. She was in the garden in Honfleur, sitting on the big swing under the old pine tree, and was swinging as high as she could, as my son stood behind her and pushed. Each time, he yelled: 'Higher, Giulietta, higher!'

*

A few days later, I left the house for the first time in two weeks. An azure May sky was stretched across Paris, and the trees and flowers were in full bloom in the parks. The sun shone warmly on my face, and in my jacket was stuck a long letter I had written to Hélène over the weekend. Although I'd been sick, there were still several things I could share with her.

I stepped onto the Metro, where today's passengers seemed less grouchy than usual. I gazed down at my bright spring bouquet, looking forward to placing it on Hélène's grave.

The Cimetière Montmartre was a verdant paradise where nature had exploded over the past few weeks. The birds were chirping in the trees, and the scent of chestnut blossoms filled the air.

I drank in the mild air as I walked along, and I soon reached the small path at the end of the cemetery where visitors rarely appeared. The last time I'd been here, Arthur had been with me, and Sophie had been working on her angel close by. Obviously, the restoration job was finished, since the stone angel now had both of its wings and was gazing peacefully at the grave it was tending. On the other hand, Sophie was nowhere in sight.

It was only a few steps further to Hélène's grave, and for a moment I stared despondently at the bronze angel's dear face.

'I hope you aren't upset at me any more, Hélène,' I murmured, thinking about that last frantic letter that I had deposited over two weeks ago. 'It's been a while since you've heard from me. I've been ill.'

I searched for a vase for my flowers behind the gravestone, and took a step back to admire how tenderly and brightly they glowed against the ivy. I then pulled the letter out of my jacket, pressed the catch on the back of the gravestone, and opened the secret compartment. As usual, I leaned down to place the envelope on top of the other letters, but froze in mid-bend.

I couldn't believe my eyes, but there was no doubt about it.

The secret compartment was empty. All the letters were gone.

And in their place sat a small stone heart.

12

More things in heaven and earth

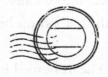

For the past hour, I'd been sitting on the steps of the Sacré-Cœur, gazing out at the city spread below me. Under a cloudless sky, Paris shone in the midday sun. I was surrounded by life: students encamped across the wide, pale steps as they unpacked their baguettes from their backpacks; tourists clustered further down the hill, uncertain if they wanted to have their photos taken against the ornate white church glittering atop Montmartre or with the magnificent backdrop of the city behind them; couples kissing, content just to be here at this iconic locale high above the city – the epitome of romance for so many people. I too had strolled here one evening with Hélène, had sat beside her on these very steps. It had been quiet then, the city below us a sea of lights.

I opened my hand, which was still clutching the stone heart, and stared at it in disbelief, as the strangest thoughts swirled through my mind.

I had stood at the grave for a long time after discovering that my letters were gone, pressing the stone heart against my chest as I stared at the angel. I felt like I'd been struck by lightning.

'My God,' I whispered as my heart hammered loudly. 'Did you do this, Hélène?'

I eventually set my new letter in the secret compartment – looking around before I did so – and shut the little door. And then I left the cemetery, without glancing either right or left. I wandered through the streets of Montmartre like a person possessed – aimless, helpless, too agitated to take a seat in one of the cafés. As if of their own accord, my feet had found the path that led up here to the highest point in Montmartre.

Once again, I studied the heart nestled in my palm. It wasn't one of those rose-covered stone hearts you can sometimes find in gift shops. This was more like a simple stone – a shimmering pink – whose natural shape resembled that of a somewhat slanted heart. The kind of stone you might catch sight of, glowing under the burbling surface of a mountain stream, before you happily fish it out and bear it home like a treasure.

I tightened my fingers around the heart and gazed at the horizon, which had grown blurry in the noon haze. *Was it possible?* I wondered. Under these special, unique and incomprehensible – at least, by me – circumstances, was this the answer I had pleaded for so ardently in my last letter? Had Hélène sent me a sign? What else could this heart mean except love, eternal love?

I took a deep breath. *You have to calm down, Julien. Just think this all through.* I ordered myself to come back down to earth. Signs from beyond the grave, really?! Stuff like that only happened in novels where time travellers pop up in outlandish situations, or coma patients manage to leave their bodies in order to rejoin the outside world. Completely ridiculous.

But . . . was it really ridiculous? Was it actually all that crazy?

All of my letters had disappeared. I had witnessed that, at least, with my own eyes. Who knew about the letters? I hadn't told anyone about them, or about the secret compartment. I thought fleetingly about Arthur, who had recently seen me stick a letter into the compartment – but Arthur hadn't been back to the cemetery since then, and who would he have told about it, anyway? No, no. I shook my head. The disappearance of the letters had to be linked to someone else.

In theory, someone might have discovered the cavity in the gravestone and taken the letters out of curiosity. But who would actually do something like that? Who would take such personal letters? From a *cemetery*?

Perhaps an author looking for a good story. I had to grin as this thought shot through my mind.

At the same time, I had seen plenty of strangers standing at Hélène's grave. Maybe there were crazy people out there who took things from graves and collected them, like those fans who stockpile autographs from their favourite musicians.

But even if somebody had stumbled across the letters and been unable to resist the temptation to take them, there was still the stone heart. Why would someone leave me a stone heart in the compartment? Who besides Hélène would do something like that?

An image of the dark-eyed girl, who knew so much about stonework and had chatted to Arthur in the graveyard, popped into my head. Could it be Sophie?

I suddenly realised how deluded I was being. Pull yourself together, Julien. What would this young, outgoing girl – *who already had a boyfriend* – have to gain by leaving heart-shaped gifts for a depressed, middle-aged widower? The idea was ridiculous. Dismissing it from my mind, I continued to mull over the possibilities. And the more I considered it, the more intrigued I was by the idea that it was Hélène who had left me this heart as an answer. With this token, she wanted to show me that she had forgiven me for the incident with Cathérine and that she still loved me.

I gazed up into the sky, and as I sat there on the steps of the Sacré-Cœur everything suddenly seemed completely logical. Shakespeare's Danish prince said: *There are more things in heaven and earth, Horatio, than are dreamt of in your philosophy.* On this sunny day in May, the concept made more sense to me than it had back then to Hamlet.

There are so many things that happen every day that nobody can explain, I added silently. Sightings of the Virgin Mary. Mirrors that crash off walls whenever someone dies. Two parted lovers who return at the same moment to the bridge where they had first met. Even Albert Einstein, undoubted genius that he was, said that according to the laws of physics, it was possible to travel through time. If you really thought about it, it was obvious that we really had no idea what possibilities actually did exist between heaven and earth. We were only humans with a limited perspective of the horizon. Who knew what might lie beyond?

I held the heart in my hand, feeling perplexed and inspired by the miracle of it. Then a shadow fell over me.

A young woman with red hair and freckles was standing in front of me. She was wearing jeans and a light blue T-shirt bearing the words *Getting better and worse at the same time*, and was holding out her phone, as if she had a call for me from the universe.

'Would you?' she asked in a charming accent, smiling at me.

'Would I what?' I replied in confusion, staring at her as if she were some strange apparition. 'Who's on it?'

She gazed at me in astonishment, before shaking her head and laughing.

'Ha ha ha ... No. I mean, could you take a picture of me, Monsieur?'

'Oh, yes ... of course,' I stammered. 'Sorry about that.'

Good grief, I'd been a million miles away. I tucked the stone heart in my pocket and took her phone, which was already in camera mode.

The girl climbed up a few steps and stood in front of the church, whose snowy white dome towered up into the blue sky.

'But you need to get all of the Sacré-Cœur on it,' she called, posing jauntily for a few shots.

'*Merci beaucoup*,' she said afterwards, scrolling through the photos. 'Yes, very nice. Lovely!' She glanced up. 'Say ... are you from around here?'

I nodded.

'Great! Could you perhaps tell me the easiest way to get from here to Le Consulat ... I mean, the restaurant ...' She hurriedly pulled a city map out of her bag, and as she did so a small book tumbled out.

We both bent down to pick it up and almost bumped heads.

'Oh,' I said as I handed her the book. 'Do you read poetry?'

'Yes,' she said, holding the small poetry volume to her chest. 'I love Jacques Prévert. I'm writing my bachelor thesis about him and I'm spending a semester here in Paris. Do you know his poem about the garden? "Le Jardin"? It's so wonderful ...'

Her eyes sparkled, and I felt struck by the coincidence.

'Of course I know it,' I replied. Anyone who has ever been young and in love eventually stumbles across that poem – the most beautiful lines that have ever been written about a kiss. 'Who doesn't?'

As if following a secret script, I almost asked the young student if she might like to join me for a cup of coffee. However, she spoke up faster: 'Where is Le Consulat? I'm supposed to meet someone there in a few minutes.'

We leaned over the map, and I showed her the way.

'If you go along there, you can't miss it,' I called after her as she sprinted up the steps of the Sacré-Cœur.

She turned around.

'Thank you, Monsieur. And I hope you have a nice day!'

'Hey, wait a second! What's your name?'

I knew it was stupid, but half of me expected her to say 'Hélène', or even 'Helen', considering her English accent.

'Caroline,' she called back with a laugh before she disappeared.

A few minutes later, I was meandering down the street that ran past Le Consulat when I caught sight of her sitting in the sunshine. She was laughing with a young man. She didn't notice me when I walked past her, and I found myself amazed by how strangely circular life can be. Events repeated themselves and everything was connected. I wasn't really a person who believed in signs, but after a day like this, Doubting Thomas would have believed in the Resurrection.

Of course, I couldn't know *for sure* if the heart-shaped stone in my pocket truly was a sign. Nonetheless, like the bird in the proverb who believes that the sun will rise even before daybreak, I believed it was exactly that.

In any case, my encounter with the red-haired student had given me
an idea. When I got back home, I rummaged around my bookshelves
until I located the poem by Jacques Prévert. Then I sat down at my
desk and wrote my next letter to Hélène.

My Most Beloved,

*The fourteenth of May will, from this day forward, be
especially significant to me. Starting on this day – today – I
once again believe that you will be with me always, my angel.
Just as you promised me when I was lying in bed with a fever
and I dreamed about you. You are more than just a body lying in
a cemetery, slowly rejoining the earth. You exist somewhere. The
fact that someone dies doesn't necessarily mean that they are no
longer here.*

*I went to the Cimetière Montmartre today in order to
bring you a letter once again, after all these weeks. But I was
astonished to find that the secret compartment was empty.
Instead of the small pile of letters which had been building up
over the weeks, I discovered a stone heart. It's sitting here in
front of me as I write, and despite all rational explanation,
I defiantly hope it is from you, my beloved. The last time I
wrote to you, I wished so hard to receive an answer from you,
just once. Remember? And now, I can almost believe that I've
received just that.*

*When I caught sight of the empty compartment today and
discovered the stone heart there, my own heart stopped, Hélène.
I was speechless. In fear, in delight. I strolled through the streets
of Montmartre, trying to understand what had just happened.*

My heart raced for joy, but then I began to wonder. Something like this wasn't actually possible. Was it? My heart, which wanted so much to believe, and my head, which knew better, struggled for the upper hand. As I wheezed up the old hill, I was caught between 'impossible' and 'perhaps possible', and when I reached the top I met a red-haired girl on the steps of the Sacré-Cœur who reminded me so much of you. She adores poetry, just like you, although she prefers Prévert to Heine. As we chatted, it seemed I was caught in a dialogue I knew already, and I suddenly had the feeling I was the hero of a time-travel story. This time, though, the red-haired student didn't have coffee with me, but with a young man. At Le Consulat of all places, Hélène!

And at that moment, my heart won out.

I don't understand how everything is connected, my love. All I know is that we have May, and that somehow – however impossible – I have found you again. I have you again, as once in May.

And I'm sending you this greeting with all my love, which is as eternal as that kiss in the Montsouris Park that Prévert captured for all time – for us and for everyone who has ever been in love!

Julien

The Garden

Millennia upon millennia
Will not suffice
To explain the brief moment of eternity

When you kissed me
When I kissed you
One morning in winter's light
In Parc Montsouris in Paris
In Paris
On this Earth
Which is a star.

13

Feeling better and worse at the same time

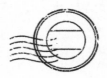

Alexandre came by that evening. Usually I would have been glad to see him, but I suspected that spending time with him today was not the best of ideas.

My hunch turned out to be right. My friend might curse like a sailor, but he is remarkably sensitive to even the smallest of changes in those around him. Alexandre had hardly stepped through the door when his radar pinged.

'What's going on? You seem different,' he declared as he tugged off his trench coat. He studied me through narrowed eyes.

'Nothing's going on,' I replied. 'Come in.'

I tried to present a neutral face. Frankly, I felt like I was about to burst with the news about what had happened earlier. I would have loved to tell someone about it all – the missing letters, the stone heart, my impossible theory – but I knew without a doubt that Alexandre would start trying to reel me back down to earth as soon as I started telling him my story. The goldsmith might enjoy creating pieces of jewellery that made women dream, but both of his feet were planted firmly on the ground. Which is more than I could say about myself. Besides, I felt a certain reluctance to disclose anything about the letters I'd been writing. It was the last secret I shared with Hélène, and who knew what might happen if I let the word get out?

And so we sat in the living room, and I opened a bottle of wine. Alexandre told me about an American couple who had bought out half of his stock today, and then he asked about the 'pretty neighbour'. I was able to report that Cathérine had taken everything in her stride, and had even teamed up with me against the old battleaxe downstairs. We sipped our red wine, and I lit one cigarette after the other, feeling transparent as I did so. My thoughts kept drifting, but I did my best to pretend that I was actually listening.

'Julien? Hello? Are you still with me?' Alexandre snapped his fingers in front of my face, and I almost jumped out of my seat. 'Well, what do you think?'

I stared at him. I had no idea what he wanted from me.

Before I could respond, he started talking again.

'You aren't saying anything because you haven't been listening! And don't even try to tell me that nothing's changed. Something's happened, I can feel it. You aren't sitting here like a sleepwalker for no reason.' He fixed his dark eyes on me and stared hard, then suddenly laughed.

'Come on ... No, it's impossible ...' He shook his head in disbelief, and for a moment, I thought he had guessed everything. 'You haven't . . . There's no way you've . . . *fallen in love?*'

'*What?!*' I sat straight up in my chair and forcefully stubbed out my cigarette. 'No, of course *not*, you idiot!'

'Whoa!' He lifted his hands appeasingly. 'It's all good, no worries. But you have to tell me what's going on. Come on,' he coaxed. 'Tell your old Jim.'

I had to laugh, then bit my lip.

He scooted around in his chair in anticipation and leaned toward me. 'I get it. You have a secret. Is it something good, at least? You don't seem quite as down as before, so that's something.'

'I wish I knew,' I said, recalling the words on the red-haired student's T-shirt. 'Feeling better and worse at the same time,' I murmured.

'What are you babbling about? You're speaking in riddles, *mon ami*. Could you be a little more specific? What do you mean, you feel both better and worse at the same time?'

I exhaled loudly and slid a little further back into the upholstery.

'You wouldn't believe the day I've just had,' I began with a sigh, sending a quick prayer up to Hélène.

And then I told him everything.

I have to hand it to Alexandre. He didn't interrupt me even once. He occasionally sniffed in disapproval, after which he would take a sip of wine, then return to gazing at me thoughtfully and sympathetically. And once I reached the end of my story, he did exactly what I'd been afraid he would do. He tore everything apart.

'Man, oh man,' he said, shaking his head in utter disbelief. 'Now you've really lost it, Julien. As you were talking, couldn't you hear how wild it all sounded?'

At the moment, all I felt was regret that I had told him anything at all.

'I knew you wouldn't see it my way,' I said. 'But there are more things in heaven and earth ...'

'Esoteric shit,' he cut in.

'That esoteric shit happens to be from Shakespeare,' I declared smugly.

'You might not believe it, but I happen to know that already. But – hey, Julien! Wake up! Hélène was a wonderful woman. She was the best, and she will always exist in here, unforgotten.' He tapped his heart. 'But she is *dead*, Julien! She *can't* take letters out of gravestones or drop off stone hearts for anyone.'

I leaped up and marched as resolutely as any general through the open French doors to the back part of the living room, where my desk sat against the wall. I grabbed the stone heart, walked back, and waved it in front of Alexandre's puzzled face.

'Then what is this?' I asked.

'My God, Julien, pull yourself together! This is completely absurd, can't you see that? Listen to yourself. A sign from Hélène! Where are we? In *Poltergeist II* or *Ghost*?'

He took the heart from me and studied it from all angles, shaking his head. He then set it down with a sigh on the coffee table.

'I'm beginning to get really worried about you, Julien. To be honest, the whole thing with the letters seems borderline to me – a secret compartment in a gravestone takes some getting used to – but it's fine if it helps, and you promised her you'd do it. Hélène was smart. She had something in mind when she asked you to do that. However, it would be best if you focused your activities on people made of flesh and blood and not – excuse me for putting it bluntly – on a body that's crumbling away.' His eyes were concerned. 'That seems twisted all the way around. You can't keep sleeping with the dead.'

I crossed my arms and decided to ignore his insults.

'Where'd the heart come from, then?' I insisted, confronting him with the hard facts. 'Who took the letters?'

Alexandre shrugged. 'I wish I knew,' he said. 'It definitely wasn't Hélène. I'm sorry, my friend, but I'd bet my right arm on that.'

'Your risk, not mine,' I replied as he grinned.

'Just give it some time.'

Neither of us said anything for a few moments. Down on the street, a car revved its engine as it drove by. My thoughts turned back to Hélène and the letter I would drop off tomorrow. *And then we'll see*, I thought stubbornly. *Then we'll see!*

But what did I honestly expect? Another answer? That the head of the bronze angel would start speaking to me? I sighed, and Alexandre glanced over at me.

'You have to stop this nonsense, Julien. You're running yourself into the ground with it.' He picked up the bottle and topped up our glasses. 'Believe me, I'd be the first one to shout from the rooftops if Hélène could come back to life. But that won't happen.' He leaned forward, pushing away my hand which was already reaching for the cigarettes again. 'And you can't keep going through those so fast. This place is as smoky as an Irish pub. Do you want to kill your child while you're at it?' He strode over to the window and opened it. The cool air streamed inside.

'Ahhh!' Alexandre cried. *'Aspirez, aspirez!'* He inhaled deeply before joining me on the sofa. 'Look, Julien, even if you *were* right – even if Hélène *did* take the letters and leave behind the heart – what good would that do?'

'Then I'd know she was still out there,' I said quietly.

'But, Julien, you already know that, at least as long as you want to believe it. So okay, let's assume she's out there somewhere, like you say. Who knows? Maybe it's really true, and this very second she's sitting on that empty chair over there, listening to every word we say. Or she's invisibly flitting around us like the dead characters in that play by Sartre – what's it called?'

'*No Exit.*'

'That's it, thanks! All right, just for argument's sake, everything you say is true. What do you gain from it? In a concrete sense? Can you sit with Hélène on the couch and chat? Can you feel her or hold her? Can she lie next to you in bed every night? Can you eat breakfast together in the morning, while you tell her about what you've read in the paper? Can she laugh when Arthur says something funny? Can she stand in the kitchen and make her divine *clafoutis aux cerises* for you? No, none of these things will happen, Julien.' He watched me. 'Is that what you're thinking? Do you really think that some day she's going to waltz in here with a daisy wreath on her head and take you into her arms?'

I lowered my head and stared dejectedly at the stone heart.

'But who . . . ?' I asked helplessly. I picked up the pink stone and clung to it like a diamond.

Alexandre placed his arm around my shoulders. 'Julien. Do you really think I don't know how hard this all is for you?' he said.

And we sat once again in silence, as the window clattered softly in the night wind.

'I have to admit it's all very strange,' he finally conceded. 'But I am certain there's a simple explanation for this "miracle".' He flicked air quotes and seemed to be thinking. 'Did Arthur perhaps tell someone about the secret compartment?'

I shook my head. 'No, I asked him about it when I put him to bed. He couldn't even remember what it was I was talking about. He'd forgotten already. His mind is filled with his own stuff, like his crush on a red-haired girl in his nursery school.' I couldn't help but smile, remembering how Arthur had pointed out his little friend when I had picked him up from the nursery.

'Isn't she pretty, Papa?' he had whispered.

'He clearly has your genes,' Alexandre remarked drily. Then he straightened up suddenly.

'Of course, that's it!' He slapped his hand to his forehead. 'Why didn't I think of that right away? It's so obvious. The stonemason!'

'The stonemason?! Now you're the crazy one, Alexandre! The *stonemason* took my letters and left me a heart – clear as day! The stonemason, whose wife and two grown sons are in business with him, discovered in his old age that he has a thing for young widowers – that's a good one. Ha, ha, ha!'

'No, wait a minute!' Alexandre had picked up a scent and refused to be put off. 'The stonemason who you ordered the gravestone from is the only person who definitely knows about the compartment.' He thought for a moment. 'It wouldn't have to be the stonemason himself. It could be someone in his workshop – or perhaps the master boasted about it to someone, like another client. Who knows? Maybe somewhere out there, an unhappy widow is flitting around who thinks that your idea of the secret compartment is the greatest act of romantic sentiment she has ever heard of. And so she decided to stop by to see what solemn offerings you were leaving behind for your wife. And then she found the letters, all of which she read, of course. Women are like that. Curious and incorrigibly romantic.'

'Hmm,' I was dumbfounded. 'You know what, Alexandre? *You* should be the one writing the novels.' I was impressed with how deftly he had conjured up this theory. And I had to admit that there could be something to his story about the stonemason. The man did like to talk – a lot. I remembered feeling a little annoyed by that the day I'd picked out the gravestone.

'No, I'll leave the writing to you,' Alexandre replied, flattered. 'But I'd be happy to let you use this splendid idea for your next novel.' He grinned contentedly, since the evening was ending on a note that both of us could live with. He then drained his glass and set it firmly down on the table.

'I'm telling you, follow up on that guy.' He chuckled. 'And it wouldn't hurt to keep an eye out for pretty widows around the cemetery, especially ones hanging out near the grave. I think that's the ticket, old chum.'

'I'll do that, Alexandre, promise,' I said. 'I wanted to go to the cemetery tomorrow, anyway. I wrote another letter. We'll see if that one disappears, too.'

'We'll see,' Alexandre declared. 'Stay vigilant, my friend. You'll figure out soon enough who's behind this.'

I nodded, but as I closed the door behind him I felt strangely uneasy. Wrapped in my own thoughts, I carried our glasses into the kitchen and peeked in on Arthur, who was sleeping peacefully in his bed, his teddy bear clutched at his side. I then returned to the living room and stood at the open window. I gazed into the dark night sky, and my heart tightened.

14

He loves me, he loves me not

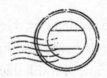

The inexplicable changes people. Questions without answers are harder to bear than anything else, and this explains why we go to great lengths to acquire certainty. We strive for truth and understanding – but what about those times when we don't really want to know what we will eventually discover? When the illusion bursts like a rainbow bubble?

The following afternoon, as I stepped through the gate of the Cimetière Montmartre, I felt quite strange. My night had been unsettled, and I had no idea what I should wish for – that my last letter would once again be missing, or that it would be peacefully sitting in the gravestone. That there would be a new sign, or that there wouldn't be even the slightest hint that someone had opened the compartment.

No one was around at this lunchtime hour. The groundskeeper was the only person to shuffle past me as I strode along the familiar path through the blooming cemetery. Alexandre had planted the seed of doubt in my heart, and as the old man growled a greeting in my direction, I peered at him closely and wondered for a moment if this odd fellow might be capable of playing such a bizarre trick on me. Perhaps he resented people, like me, who entered his stony kingdom uninvited. I glanced around a few times, and had the funny feeling that someone was following me, or that somewhere among the trees, a woman in a black veil was hiding. I wasn't blind to how strange I was starting to get.

When I finally reached Hélène's grave, my heart was racing, and I almost didn't open the compartment. But I had to.

I opened the door and felt around for the letter I had dropped off yesterday. It wasn't there, but my fingers closed around something soft. I gave a low cry, thinking it was a hand, but when I pulled out the object I laughed in relief.

It was a little wreath of forget-me-nots and daisies.

I held it, unsure what to make of it. I studied it closely, spreading the flowers apart carefully to see if perhaps a note was concealed among them, but there wasn't. Only flowers. *Only?* While I was away, someone had taken my letter and left the wreath as a sign of something.

Someone?

The first thing that came to mind when I saw the flowers was the forget-me-not nosegays from Cathérine. I still remembered vividly running into her weeks ago, when I had brought my first letter. She had admitted that the forget-me-nots were from her. And she had been rather embarrassed, as had I. Was it possible that she had seen something even back then ... that she'd been secretly watching me? I tried to recall the details of that encounter. No, there hadn't been anyone close to the grave – I would have noticed. And why would she do something this crazy? Cathérine lived in the same building as I did. She could talk to me whenever she wanted, so she wouldn't need to lurk around cemeteries and open gravestones. Besides, it occurred to me that she had been at school all day yesterday, and Arthur had spent the whole afternoon at her place, playing with Zazie. The cemetery was locked every evening at six o'clock, and I couldn't imagine Cathérine scaling the tall green iron gate after nightfall in order to leave off more forget-me-nots.

I shook my head.

'Julien, you're seeing ghosts!' I chided myself.

And truly I was, because suddenly I felt as if I could see Hélène's handiwork clearly in the wreath. In my dream, hadn't she been wearing a wreath of daisies?

'Oh, Hélène, what are you up to?' I whispered dazedly, watching the angel, which didn't move a centimetre. 'I don't know what to believe any more.'

I pulled out the letter with the Prévert poem from my satchel and placed it in the cavity.

'I look forward to seeing if you like this,' I whispered as I closed the compartment.

I then took a step back and examined the gravestone thoroughly. To the uninformed eye, the hairline crack that marked the opening was hardly visible.

I knew it was all quite extraordinary, but as I stood there at the grave with the wreath of flowers in my hand and my gaze fixed on Hélène's face, I felt separated from the world. The force of Alexandre's arguments faded.

I tore myself reluctantly away, abandoned the narrow paths, and slowly strolled down the Avenue Hector Berlioz. But then I heard my name.

I looked up and caught sight of a dark, delicate figure, sitting on a bench a short distance away, almost lost among the tall, steep-roofed family mausoleums. Her tool bag beside her, she was taking a lunch break.

'*Salut*, Julien!' Sophie called cheerfully. 'Well? Back again? I haven't seen you in ages.'

'I was here yesterday, actually,' I replied, and she cocked her eyebrows in astonishment. 'But I was sick.'

'And here I thought you had decided to rejoin the living, and I wouldn't ever see you again.' She straightened her cap, as her eyes sparkled impishly.

If you only knew, little pixie, if you only knew, I thought.

'I would've been disappointed if you had,' she added with a grin. 'To be honest, I was starting to miss our cemetery chats.' She slid a little to one side. 'Come and join me for a minute. I was just eating lunch. How are you doing?'

'Oh ... well ... as good as could be expected,' I stammered, staring at the wreath I was still holding. 'Considering the circumstances.' I shrugged.

'Pretty flowers,' she said abruptly. 'Are they for your wife?'

'No, no. I was already at the grave,' I replied before thinking better of it. I almost bit my tongue when she glanced over at me in surprise.

'Who are the flowers for then?'

'The flowers ... uh ... The flowers ...' I sounded like an idiot. 'The flowers are for you!' My heart dropped as soon as the words came out of my mouth. I knew it was silly, that they weren't really from Hélène, but all the same I felt a pang at giving them away.

'For *me*?' A pale blush spread across her face. 'But . . .'

'Yes,' I hurried to add, depositing the wreath on her lap a little hastily, trying to disguise my reaction. 'I had hoped we would run into each other. You might not believe it, but I missed you, too.' I laughed and added jokingly: 'After all, you were the one who said that flowers are wasted on graves, or something like that.'

'Good memory, author,' she said, laughing in response, although her eyes were doubtful. She brushed a few baguette crumbs from her overalls. 'So . . . are they really for me?' she asked again.

I nodded eagerly. 'Yes, of course, like I said!'

'You really are good at inventing stories,' she replied. 'Nonetheless, thank you!' She set the wreath beside her.

'Forget-me-nots and daisies,' she added thoughtfully. 'Do you know what they mean in the language of flowers?'

'No, what?'

'Well . . . Forget-me-nots stand for love and fidelity. Long ago, people used to say that the eyes of new lovers resembled the colour of forget-me-nots . . . ' She looked into my eyes. 'Oh . . . *yes!*' she crowed. 'Your eyes really are as blue as forget-me-nots.'

She grinned as I smiled, feeling ill at ease suddenly. What was this? Was she flirting with me?

'What else?' She picked a daisy from the wreath and held it up. 'The daisy represents genuine happiness. Isn't that lovely? Do you know what else you can do with a daisy?' She waved the flower in front of my face. 'Well?'

I had to laugh. 'No clue. Tell me. I'm not as acquainted with the language of flowers.'

'Oh, come on, Julien. Every child knows the old game!' She started to pluck the flower petals. 'He loves me . . . he loves me not . . . he loves me . . . he loves me not.' She continued until only one petal remained. 'He loves me not! What a shame!' She tossed the stem over her shoulder before looking at me closely. 'Don't you want to tell me what's really going on with the pretty wreath? Or is it some kind of secret? I *love* secrets.' She smiled when I didn't respond. 'All right, something easier: How's everything going with the book, author?'

No, not flirting at all.

'So so,' I quipped. I looked at her, and then I had an idea. 'And you, Sophie? I saw that the angel has new wings. Is your work coming along well? Must be better than mine. What are you working on right now?'

'Oh, at the moment I'm restoring the inscription on a family vault. Not particularly challenging for a stonemason, but a job's a job.'

I nodded knowingly, even though I knew as little about sculpture projects as the dog did about the moon when he was howling at it. 'Hey, Sophie, you're here every day, right?'

'Well, *almost* every day. I sometimes take the weekends off. There's more to life than angels and gravestones, don't you think?' She picked up her ham sandwich and took a hearty bite from it. 'For example, today I'll be calling it quits earlier than usual. It's my cousin's birthday, and we've been invited over later.'

I didn't ask who 'we' was. Instead, I asked as casually as I possibly could: 'In the past few days, have you happened to notice anyone around Hélène's grave? Besides me, I mean.'

Her eyes were curious, but she shrugged.

'Hmm,' she said. 'I'll have to think . . .' She began to tick them off. 'The groundskeeper cleared the pathway. I also recall that a group of Japanese tourists took pictures of several graves. I think the bronze angel was one of them. An elegant gentleman also came by, as well as a woman in a large black hat and a small older lady.' She paused to think. 'Some blonde woman keeps coming by with flowers, too.'

The blonde woman had to be Cathérine.

'Anyone else?' I asked.

'Good grief! You want a lot of details. What for? Are you wanting to test your wife's popularity rating? Anyway, I don't see everything, of course, but I'd say that her grave is visited more often than others, excluding the celebrities.' She wrinkled her forehead. 'Who else? I saw a couple standing for a long time at the grave. They examined everything quite closely, and the man was even jotting down notes in a little book – but that was a while ago. And – oh, I saw a *clochard* totter around near the grave with his bottle of red wine a few days ago.' She grimaced a little.

'And yesterday? Did you see anybody yesterday?'

She shook her head. 'Sorry, but no. I mean, somebody might have been around there, but if so, I didn't see them because I was too far away.'

'And when you were working close to Hélène's grave, on that angel back then – did one of those people, uh, do something to the grave?'

Her eyes looked puzzled. 'What do you mean by *do something*, Julien?' she asked. 'Vandalism? Has something been damaged or stolen?'

I could feel my cheeks grow warm. Maybe I should just tell her the whole truth, but I didn't. Sophie was bound to think I was every bit as crazy as my friend Alexandre did.

'Uh, no,' I said quickly. 'I mean, yes. I'm missing my watering can. I keep it behind the gravestone.'

'Aha.' I wasn't sure if she really believed me. For a moment, her eyes – large and round – rested on me. 'So, grave robbers,' she added with a smile and a click of her tongue. 'Well, if you like, I'll keep an eye out for you, Julien. I'm always here.'

Her phone rang, and she shot me an apologetic look.

'No, no,' I assured her, as I stood up and waved goodbye. 'Take it. I have to go, anyway.'

Sophie smiled in farewell and gestured cheerfully once more at the wreath. As I walked away, I heard her voice take on a softer note: 'No, of course, I haven't forgotten, *Chouchou*. I'm wrapping up here soon like I said ... Yes, yes, I'll be back home no later than five ... Yes ... Love you, too.'

And so I left the cemetery empty-handed, in the truest sense of the phrase. My subsequent visit to Bertrand & Fils, Gravestones and More didn't shed much more light – at least, not in terms of Alexandre's theory about the pretty widow with a romantic streak.

I discovered Monsieur Bertrand outside among his gravestones. He was in the middle of a consultation with an older couple, holding forth on the advantages of using recycled headstones.

'We could smooth out the old inscription, and replace it with something new and pretty,' he proclaimed loudly. 'That won't cost as much in the long run, but it will still look nice. No one would ever need to know that the stone had been used before.' He scratched behind his ear and glanced over in my direction. 'But look around as you like. As I always say, looking doesn't cost a thing.'

The couple started to make their way through the displayed gravestones, sunk in quiet debate, as Monsieur Bertrand walked toward me with a smile. He obviously recalled me at once.

'Monsieur Azoulay! What brings you back to me?' He shook my hand. 'I hope you aren't in the market for another gravestone so soon.'

I was able to quickly assuage his concern.

Standing in the noon sun among all the unworked stones, I awkwardly explained my visit.

Monsieur Bertrand's reaction was swift and emotional. I had obviously insulted his professional honour.

'Now, listen to me!' he exclaimed indignantly, spreading his arms in a gesture of innocence. 'You actually think I'd do that? I don't know what to say.' He kept shaking his head in disbelief. 'Young man, I've been running this business for over forty years, and my father ran it before me. And when I'm dead and buried, which hopefully won't be the case any time soon' – he rapped a marble pedestal standing nearby – 'my sons will take over the business ... But no one has ever—' He gazed at me reproachfully. 'No one has ever filed a complaint.'

'I'm not filing a complaint, either,' I quickly replied. 'I was only wondering if perhaps you had found yourself in a situation in which you told somebody about the ... uh ... *uniqueness* of the gravestone.' I lowered my voice.

Monsieur Bertrand sniffed. 'If that did happen, please just tell me,' I whispered. 'It is critical for me to know if someone is aware of its unusual nature. It's a matter of life and death, you might say.' I stared hard at him, satisfied at having come up with a suitable metaphor.

The stonemason took a step back, shutting his eyes in alarm. But then he returned my gaze without even the slightest flinch, lacing his fingers together over the work apron that spanned his generous stomach.

'Absolutely not, Monsieur Azoulay. I built that compartment myself – me personally – I didn't even allow my sons to help. At the time, you told me to handle the matter confidentially, which is what I did. I haven't told a soul – the devil take me if that's not the truth! The things that pass between me and the customer never leave this workshop. You can believe me on that. You'd be shocked at the kinds of stories I've heard. Or the peculiar wishes that survivors sometimes have.'

He rolled his eyes dramatically, and I chose not to pursue this line of thought.

'No, no, Monsieur, discretion is our business. I'm always telling my sons that. Discretion to the grave and beyond. I'm not only a stonemason, I can also be as silent as the grave. Hahaha!' He laughed loudly. He probably trotted out this old chestnut with some frequency, considering it almost sounded like a slogan. 'The silent-as-the-grave stonemason.'

The couple, who were still strolling among the polished blocks of stone, stopped chatting and glanced over at us with interest.

When Monsieur Bertrand noticed I wasn't laughing with him, he tried again. 'More like *two* graves, hahaha!' His massive stomach shuddered.

Such a high concentration of mirth among all the gravestones was a little too much for me. I made my exit and left Monsieur Bertrand to his new customers, who would doubtlessly soon benefit for all eternity from his discretion.

15

At the forest's edge of memory

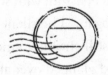

When Alexandre called on Sunday morning, I was absentmindedly paging through the yellowing pages of a small antiquarian poetry volume, published by Librairie Gallimard, as I'd done often in recent days. They were filled with Prévert's wonderful poems – and a few of the lines in this small book were obviously intended for me, though I was puzzled by several of them.

Yes, I had been to Hélène's grave again – curiosity propelled me. And yes, my previous letter had disappeared like the others. When I deposited my new envelope in the compartment, I found this old volume of poetry. I pulled it out, amazed, delighted, bewildered.

This old, somewhat worn paperback, which resembled – maybe a *trouvaille* from the book stalls of the *bouquinistes* who lined the bank of the Seine to sell their old treasures – was an unmistakable response to my previous letter with the Prévert poem. The one that all lovers knew.

While still at the grave, I began to leaf through the small book. A name written in somewhat old-fashioned cursive decorated the first page, but it didn't mean anything to me – Augustine Bellier. She had obviously been the book's previous owner, and had probably died long ago. I turned page after page searching for an annotation, a dog-eared page, anything that could give me a clue about the meaning behind this gift. I eventually discovered an old, uninscribed postcard decorated with white roses stuck between two pages, which was obviously functioning as a bookmark. The title of the poem on this particular page was 'Cet amour' – 'This Love'.

I didn't know it.

It was a long poem about love, which was personified in the text. What it was and how it could be. How people can sometimes forget about love, but love never forgets about us. And someone had lightly underlined the final lines in pencil.

Standing there at the grave, the words touched me deeply. And even later – after I had left the cemetery and had read the poem over and over, trying to grasp the message being conveyed to me by either a heavenly or earthly being – I had to swallow every time I reached the words, *Do not let us grow cold and stony*. And the strong pleading at the end of the poem drew tears to my eyes: *At the forest's edge of memory / Suddenly appear / Hold out your hand / And save us*.

I understood it all. Hélène, my stony angel, whom I shouldn't leave to turn cold and who continued to love me, even at the forest's edge of memory. The reference must be to the cemetery, the intersection between life and death, so to speak.

At that moment, when I discovered the Prévert volume, I knew without a doubt that there was no way Cathérine was behind all this, regardless of how often she visited the cemetery. Unlike her friend Hélène, Cathérine didn't have a poetic bone in her body. She had studied science in college, and her thesis had borne the prosaic title of *Tracking Down Microbes*. I mean – good grief! – she was a *biology teacher*. She didn't read poems. Nor did she give them as gifts. I mentally apologised to all the biology teachers who actually do read poetry. Of course, such a thing was possible. After all, Boris Pasternak had been a doctor, while also writing some of the most beautiful poems ever. But that wasn't Cathérine, my neighbour. I doubted if she even had any poetry on her rather modest bookshelves.

Thus, I was spending this particular Sunday morning in bed, slightly lost among the poet's lovely words. I was already mentally formulating my next letter to Hélène when my phone went off, jerking me out of my thoughts.

It was Alexandre, wanting to know how my visit to the stonemason had gone. 'And ... did you find out anything?'

'You need to forget about him. He swore up and down he didn't tell a soul,' I said, before giving Alexandre the details about my meeting with the discreet-to-the-grave Monsieur Bertrand.

'Well,' my friend replied. 'How can you really know if he's telling the truth?'

'Come on, Alexandre. Just drop it!' I groaned. 'No more conspiracy theories. There isn't a pretty widow somewhere who cares about my emotional health.'

'What a shame,' Alexandre declared. 'Did you find out anything else?'

I reluctantly told him about my conversation with Sophie, counting off all the people she had seen close to the grave

'Aha, we do have something, then! The woman with the black hat!' he cried triumphantly. 'That sounds a lot like a widow, to my mind. Or do you know someone else with a black hat like that?'

'Nobody. The last woman I saw in a large black hat was in a Fellini film. But since Monsieur Bertrand is as silent as the grave, this speculation is just a waste of time.'

'And the older woman the sculptor mentioned?'

'Well, I wonder if that might've been my mother. Maman goes to the cemetery occasionally, although it's not her favourite hangout.'

'Unlike you,' Alexandre said.

'Right, unlike me,' I said, peeved. 'You could've spared us both that commentary, couldn't you?'

'Sorry about that,' he replied contritely, but prodded nonetheless: 'Did you find anything in the compartment this time?'

'Yes.' My interest in this conversation was fading quickly.

'And? Don't make it so hard to wheedle stuff out of you. I just want to help.'

I sighed and told him about my last two discoveries.

As soon as he heard about the wreath, he interrupted me.

'It was the pretty neighbour, had to be! She's the one who regularly brings forget-me-nots. You told me that yourself. And the sculptor – didn't she say that a blonde woman keeps visiting the grave? Who knows? Maybe your neighbour's infatuated with you, after all.'

'Yes, Einstein, I already thought about that. But Cathérine doesn't make the shortlist of suspects for other reasons. First of all, she wasn't at the cemetery the day the wreath appeared. Secondly . . .'

'Secondly?'

I told him about the poetry book.

'Hmm,' Alexandre replied. 'Hm. Hm. Hm. That actually doesn't sound much like Mademoiselle Balland. What's the poem about?'

I explained the poem and read him the final underscored lines.

'That sounds more like Hélène, don't you think?' I asked cautiously.

'No, I don't think so,' he said. 'Not at all. The opposite, actually.'

'What do you mean?' I asked unwillingly.

And then my friend Alexandre laid out a completely different interpretation of Prévert's verses.

'Well, it's pretty straightforward,' he said. 'You shouldn't let yourself turn as cold and stony as all those gravestones, nor should you shut your heart off from a new love. Love will give you a sign – at the cemetery, which is where all your memories of Hélène keep driving you. Love will suddenly stand before you, wanting to save you if only you'll let it. It's already holding out its hand to you, understand?'

Perplexed, I didn't say anything. 'Well ...' I said, 'that's the way it is with poems. You can interpret them all sorts of ways, like the statements from the Oracle of Delphi. Anyway, I thought about Hélène straight away.'

'Why am I not surprised?' Alexandre laughed. He seemed to be enjoying this game. 'You never think about anything but Hélène, my friend.'

'And how does the stone heart fit into your theory?' I asked, disgruntled. Maybe it had been a mistake to tell Alexandre about everything that was going on

I thought about that first discovery, which was still sitting on my desk. It had started everything – the stone heart Hélène had left for me as a sign that she would love me for ever. And it couldn't have been an accident that I had received this sign at the moment I needed it the most, in the midst of my despair.

'That fits perfectly, old chum,' Alexandre replied. 'You should finally open your stony heart to life again.'

I didn't say anything. I could hear echoes of my mother talking.

'So back to Cathérine . . .' Alexandre mused. 'Or someone else who has you in their sights. What about that girl from the cemetery?'

'Sophie?'

'Could she have something to do with it? Maybe she's rather smitten with the nice young widower. After all, she spends all her time pottering around the graves.'

At the start, I had thought it might be Sophie. Sophie, who had someone to say the words 'Love you, too' to on the phone. 'No chance, she has a boyfriend,' I declared, thinking about her voice, which I had suddenly remembered as being very tender.

'How do you know that?'

'He calls her all the time. And she calls him *Chouchou* and is completely in love. Besides, she's too down-to-earth for . . . poetry.'

'Fine,' Alexandre replied, striking 'the sculptor' from his list. 'Who else do you know that reads poetry?'

'No one. Hélène.'

'Julien! Please . . . I sometimes think you're going soft in the head. What about your publisher, that . . . What's his name? Fabre?'

'Jean-Pierre Favre,' I corrected.

'Yes, what about him? The elegant gentleman standing at the grave? This Favre is bound to be super-sophisticated, a man of words and imagination – he's got to have poetry on his shelves. Maybe he's afraid you'll never finish your book and wants to lead you back to the right path.'

'And that's why he wants to attract my attention to the *cemetery*?'

'No – away from the cemetery, but you don't want to listen to me.'

'What a ridiculous idea! I might as well claim *you're* behind all this, Alexandre. After all, you're the one who engraves lines of poetry on your necklaces. I bet you've used at least one line from Prévert, right? I wouldn't put it past you.'

'Cold, freezing cold,' Alexandre said.

Neither of us said anything, and I sat in bed and plucked aimlessly at my scarf.

'Well then ...' Alexandre eventually said, and I was interested to hear what might come next.

'... the only one left is Elsa L.'

He chuckled, and this idea was so funny that I couldn't help laughing as well.

'Want to get together tonight?' Alexandre asked. 'We might come up with a better explanation.'

'No and no,' I replied. 'My mother bought tickets for a children's performance of *The Magic Flute*. We're taking Arthur to see it this afternoon.'

Maman was convinced that it was never too early to start a child's cultural education. '*The Magic Flute* is just the thing for a four-year-old,' she had insisted when she saw my arched eyebrows. 'Besides, Arthur will turn five yet this year.'

'Well, enjoy the enchantment,' my friend quipped. 'See you soon.'

My beloved Hélène, the sunshine of my night,
  I feel so torn, dear one! I want so much to believe that you're
the one taking my letters and leaving me signs, and sometimes I
believe this completely, no matter what Alexandre says.

When I discovered the Prévert poem, I was certain you had to be the one behind it – who else would give me poems? And wasn't this the perfect answer to my own poem? But then, once again, just like right now, I ended up thinking that all of this couldn't be possible. I'm writing to you, and at the same time, I'm wondering: To whom am I actually writing? Who is reading my letters? And yet, I can't stop writing them. What would the alternative be? No letters to write and no responses to receive? And besides, I promised you, dearest, and I'll keep writing and hoping until I reach the thirty-third letter. I'm just not sure what to hope for.

That I will have you again, as once in May? That my life will take a happier turn?

Back when I made you that promise, Hélène, I had no idea that writing these letters would lead me on such an adventure. This is what it has become for me – an adventure full of riddles that only Alexandre knows about. Or is there someone else who does, too?

Oh, Hélène, I don't know any more what I should wish for! No, wait, I do know. I want all this to keep going, this strange game of big questions and small answers! If I were to imagine that suddenly I'd stop finding things in the secret compartment, that everything would end, that this contact would break off – I don't know how I'd handle that! It would feel like I'd lost everything a second time.

You once told me that writing the letters would possibly help me – and you were right, my clever wife. When I write these letters to you, I feel distracted. They knit my life back together, open a new perspective, keep me going. And the prospect of finding an answer at the grave naturally heightens these feelings all the more.

It's all so crazy – I can't risk telling anyone else about what's happening. If I do, I'll be considered a candidate for psychiatric treatment. And yet, what I want to do more than anything is cry the news out to all the world: It feels like my letters are being read and there are answers for me. For me, Julien Azoulay.

All of this is saving me, Hélène. It is carrying me through the hardest experience I've ever had, and somehow it is giving me hope, however ludicrous that might seem.

On Sunday, Maman and I took Arthur to a performance of The Magic Flute. It was performed outdoors by an independent theatre group, at the Montsouris Park. A little stage had been especially constructed. It was a children's performance, but it was all so magical. We sat there enchanted, holding each other's hands – Mamie, Arthur and I. We chuckled over Papageno's mischief and Papagena's funny ideas. And we trailed along behind Pamina and Tamino, as their great love saw them through all sorts of tests and trials.

Maybe a time of tests is waiting before me, too. I want to be strong, darling, and to not lose heart. And to keep believing that everything is going to be fine. At the moment, this is all I have: my belief.

I'm waiting on a sign – a sign from you – and long to kiss you a thousand times over.

Julien

16

The shut door

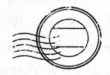

May ended, and the grief that had clapped my soul in irons turned into feverish expectation. If I had previously 'functioned', more or less, I was now overstimulated and ruled by a general nervousness that even my small son noticed.

'Papa, you keep shaking your foot,' he declared one day when we were sitting together at the kitchen table

I no longer seemed to be as numbed by unhappiness as I had been. When we went to the cinema, I even managed to follow the adventures of the young orphan boy in *My Life as a Zucchini*. Afterwards, we bought a crêpe with Nutella from a stand located on the Boulevard Saint-Germain, behind the old church.

'I'm glad you're laughing again, Papa,' Arthur declared contentedly.

During the week, I tried to write my novel, which was slowly beginning to fill with very different content than my original intention, and on the weekends I did stuff with Arthur. I occasionally met Alexandre, but I avoided talking about the vanishing letters. Whenever he asked about them, I'd crack a joke and say it was all quiet on the cemetery front.

From time to time, I even spent an evening with Cathérine on the balcony. Ever since Madame Grenouille had tarred and feathered the two of us, we had been accomplices, and the awkwardness that had existed between us since that memorable night had been displaced by a friendly, neighbourly relationship – at least, so I thought at the time.

I ate lunch at Maman's every Wednesday, and when the weather was fine, we took Arthur out to the Bois de Boulogne on Sundays. Much to his delight, we sometimes rented a rowing boat, and I would steer it across the lake, manoeuvring between the other families and the love-struck couples as he crowed and chuckled in delight. We would also occasionally take a small boat across to the Chalet des Îles in order to sit in the sun and savour a *tarte framboise*. This was the outward part of my life.

However, there was also still 'the secret', and the disquiet that had taken hold of me. It grew throughout the week, until Friday morning when Louise came to clean and I left the house to travel to that hill in the north of Paris which had obviously become my fate.

Each time I went to Montmartre, my thoughts would begin to vibrate. It felt like I was electrified. What would I find in the gravestone this time?

Because my request was always answered: the strange game with the letters and the signs had continued. I received a reply to every one of my letters. And in response to each sign, I wrote another letter. I felt like I was riding some kind of high. This feverish back and forth reminded me of the unfortunate, yet inspired, Cyrano de Bergerac, who carried on his romantic correspondence behind a façade. I longed for these small signs from the secret compartment, which I carried home like precious treasures. I would puzzle over them, interpret them. They gave me something to do. I couldn't give them up. My letters continued to vanish from the compartment, and the gravestone never failed to feed my yearning.

After I took Arthur to see *The Magic Flute*, I discovered a little music box in the gravestone. It was about the size of a matchbox and was covered in white card stock, through which you could easily make out the cut-out shapes of Papageno and Papagena, as they danced together in their feathery costumes. I excitedly turned the little crank on the side, and the mechanism played a melody:

> Risk a lot, gain a lot!
> Come, you lovely music box,
> Let the chimes ring, ring
> So they can sing.
> It sounds so lovely,
> It sounds so pretty!
> Larala la la larala la la laralala!

I placed the music box on my nightstand, and whenever I felt down in the evenings, I would pick it up and play the cheerful little song, which floated silvery through the darkness.

The next time, I found a lavender-coloured rose as an answer to my letter, followed by a glowing red pomegranate. One day, a brochure from the Musée Rodin was even sitting in the compartment.

Although Maman lived on the same street – Rue de Varenne – I had never visited this small museum, which sits in the government district, set apart a short distance from the lively Boulevard Saint-Germain. And so, one Wednesday after I had lunch at my mother's, I strolled restlessly through the magical little park that surrounds the old museum building. I circled Rodin's *Thinker*, a little baffled by the figure sunk for eternity in contemplation on his pedestal in the garden, and *The Burghers of Calais*, in their tight-knit group. I walked through the green boxwood sphere, entered the museum, and viewed the smaller works by Camille Claudel on the first floor – the woman who'd first been Rodin's pupil and then his unhappy lover, and who had created several atmospheric artworks. This had been before the great master left her and she went insane in her lovesickness, spending the rest of her days in an asylum.

I walked around the sculptures, examining their details closely. I also studied the other museum visitors through narrowed eyes and tried to figure out why I was actually here.

It is an odd feeling to search for something and to have no idea what that something is. But weren't our entire lives just such a search? The search for the 'lost land', as Henri Alain-Fournier summed it up in his *Le Grand Meaulnes*?

For a long time I stood, sunk in thought, in front of a graceful sculpture of two lovers, merging into one another and twisting to the side in a waltz step. This work, bearing the simple title *La Valse*, had been created by the unfortunate Camille, and I suddenly wondered who was leading me in my secret waltz.

I spent an hour in the Musée Rodin. After I left, I sat on a bench and was glad that I had finally come here, though I was none the wiser for my visit.

So I kept going. I wrote to Hélène without knowing if she was the one actually receiving my letters. I wanted to believe that she was, but my rational side caused me to doubt and accused me of being a hopeless idiot. At some point, I simply stopped worrying about everything. I lived inside my own world, which was like a lovely dream, and I indulged in the idea that everything would resolve itself eventually – and that is what actually happened.

However, not until much later, as summer began to wane. And only after I had finally grasped something important.

Yet during these weeks, in which spring advanced and the days grew brighter and warmer, I was left alone with my thoughts. I didn't talk much about my visits to the cemetery and my new *raison d'être*, not even with Alexandre. On the one hand, life went on – at least for everyone else. On the other hand, I had decided it was advisable to keep my secret to myself, trusting that one day I would understand everything.

The only person who couldn't help knowing about my regular visits to the Cimetière Montmartre was Sophie. Although I didn't see her every time, I was always grateful for her warm attention, her droll comments, and the jaunty way she sometimes cocked her head. Besides, she continued to inform me whenever she spotted someone at Hélène's grave. She jokingly referred to herself as my 'best spy', and agreed to occasionally join me for a cup of coffee or a glass of wine as a thank you.

These casual meetings never lasted long, and there were no repeats of supper at her favourite little bistro – the one and only time she had invited me out. All the same, I found in Sophie a friend, freely offering her thoughts and suggestions, and cheering me up when my spirits were obviously flagging.

One day, as we were having lunch together once again – this time in a street café on Rue Lepic – Sophie looked at me thoughtfully.

'May I ask you something, author?'

Uh-oh. Questions that start like this never bode well.

'Of course,' I replied as I unwrapped a sugar cube.

'Why are you so interested in who stops by Hélène's grave? Are you afraid you might have competition?' She cocked her head and pursed her lips. 'You are the undisputed champion at the cemetery, Julien. Cross my heart on that one.'

She leaned back in her chair, and a sunbeam got entangled in her hair.

I laughed in relief. But then I looked in her eyes, perhaps one heartbeat too long, and I was suddenly struck by the tempting thought that I should simply confide in this girl who seemed to be game for almost anything.

'You know, Sophie . . .'

She watched me expectantly, as my courage seeped away again. Maybe it wasn't such a good idea. Or was it? I felt myself start to flounder.

'Yes?'

'I sometimes want to tell you something, but I . . . I don't trust myself to,' I said lamely.

'Oh.' Her eyes took on a strange look, and instead of one of the sarcastic remarks that tripped so lightly across her lips, she remained silent for a long time.

I too didn't know what to say, and the awkwardness between the two of us grew with each passing minute.

'Well, just tell me whenever you *do* trust yourself,' she said.

It wasn't hard to see that she had completely misinterpreted my comment. She probably thought the idiot from the cemetery had fallen in love with her.

'No, no ... *that's* not it ...' I replied, starting to stutter. 'It ... it has nothing to do with us, Sophie,' I tried to remedy the misunderstanding. 'It is ... kind of ... a secret.'

'Ah, okay ... so, it's a secret,' she said, before we both started laughing somewhat sheepishly.

Later, whenever I thought about this strange interchange, I sometimes wondered if it had all been a misunderstanding, or if perhaps the entire truth had somehow been hidden within this misunderstanding.

Something had changed. I was no longer sad every hour, not even necessarily every day. And whether it was Sophie or my secret mission that kept leading me back to the cemetery, I had begun to shift my gaze away from old memories and to look forward once more, to the next letter, the next response, the next time.

One day in June, I found myself standing at the grave, feeling perplexed by the card I was holding. I had just swapped the card with its painted Oriental pattern from the compartment for a new letter. The card was decorated with a turquoise wooden door, surrounded by sweeping arabesques, and the door bore a quote.

> When one door to happiness closes,
> Another one opens.
> But often we gaze so long
> At the shut door
> That we fail to see
> The one that has opened for us.

I was just wondering how I should interpret this poem, when I heard the sound of quiet footsteps. I turned around and caught sight of Cathérine. She was holding a bunch of violets and watching me with interest. How long had she been standing there?

'*Salut*, Julien,' she said, taking a quick step toward me. 'What are you reading?'

'Nothing!' I quickly stuffed the card into my satchel.

She fell back a little step. 'I'm sorry. I didn't mean ... I didn't mean to pry, excuse me.'

'No, no ... it's all right. It was just ...' I left the sentence dangling in the air.

She placed her bunch of violets on the grave and smiled easily.

'It's so nice out today, and I got off of work early. So I thought I'd visit Hélène.'

'Well,' I said, smiling back. 'It looks like we both had the same idea.'

As we walked side by side down the cemetery path, I was struck by a notion.

'Hey, Cathérine ... do you know anything about this quote?'

After a moment's consideration, she shook her head. 'No, I don't think so. Is it Tagore? I only know one quote from him, which my music teacher once wrote in my autograph album. "The burden of being me becomes lighter if I can laugh at myself" – or something like that. Why do you ask?'

She had no idea. Or she was a really good actress.

'Oh, doesn't matter.'

As we walked toward the exit, we ran into Sophie, who was busy storing her tool bag in the small shed.

Sophie greeted me, ran her eyes quickly over the blonde woman walking next to me, raised her eyebrows, and gave me a telling wink. Cathérine studied the delicate dark-eyed creature in her dark cap.

Dearest Hélène,

It is Saturday evening. Earlier this afternoon, Arthur had Giulietta – a pert little girl with red hair and freckles from his nursery school – over to play for the first time. I imagine that you must have looked a lot like her when you were a child. Arthur introduced me to her after Giulietta's mother dropped her off.

He said: 'This is my Papa. He writes books.'

Giulietta was clearly impressed, and she wanted to know how long it took me to write one. If only I knew that myself! The two of them disappeared into Arthur's room, where they spent hours feverishly painting pictures. But then they were struck by the unfortunate idea of embellishing the wall over Arthur's bed. As they were doing this, I was sitting at the desk, writing away on the new novel. It will be hard for you to believe, chérie, but I'm actually making progress – not much, about three or four pages a day, but they are really good ones. I have no idea if Jean-Pierre Favre will enjoy what I'm writing, since it's turning into a very different book than what he is expecting. And will the publisher in it actually dance in the moonlight? I doubt it at this point. But the good thing is that I'm back to writing regularly.

Anyway, I was sitting there, half listening in the direction of Arthur's room where the two children were chatting and laughing a blue streak. Then everything turned quiet, with an occasional giggle or whisper thrown in. With a smile, I wondered what was going on in there, but I didn't think much more about it. At one point, I heard Arthur say: 'Let's use that one. It'll go better,' and Giulietta squealed back: 'Oh yes!' and then, in a tone that reflected knowledge of doing something quite forbidden: 'But we shouldn't do that.' I then slipped over to the bedroom and cautiously opened the door. I couldn't believe my eyes!

The two of them were standing calmly on Arthur's bed, eagerly fingerpainting the white ingrain wallpaper. The little pots of fingerpaint were practically empty.

'What are you doing?' I cried in shock.

'We wanted to paint a really, really big picture, Papa,' Arthur declared innocently, as he wiped his smeared hands on his trousers. 'Together! But the paper was too small for that.'

'We made art!' Giulietta cried, her eyes glowing. She looked like a little Papagena in her paint-spattered dress.

I gazed at the bright suns, trees, flowers, clouds, birds, and people, and suddenly I couldn't help laughing. Some of Miró's works didn't look much different from this.

'This one's Giulietta … and that's me,' Arthur announced, pointing at two figures with giant heads and tiny bodies, who were laughing with wide mouths and small pointed teeth.

They had round, spiral eyes, boxy feet, and four fingers per hand. One of the figures had bright red hair that sprang out from its head in wiry curls, crowned with a giant pink bow.

I'm not exaggerating when I say that the figures looked like Martians. However, the two names that had been written in spidery letters underneath the figures were unmistakably sublime, despite their deviation from their standard forms.

ATUR + JULETA

'Wow!' I said, for lack of anything better.

'See, Giulietta, my Papa thinks it's cool.'

They both stared at me expectantly.

I decided to be the cool father and to accept what had happened with as much composure as I could muster. With a sigh, I dug out fresh clothes from the closet for the two young artists, and I informed Arthur that I didn't want to find similar murals on any other walls in the apartment. And then I ordered pizza for us all.

As I put Arthur to bed that evening, he declared: 'That was a wonderful day, Papa.' He looked at me with sparkling eyes and sighed contentedly. 'Giulietta had fun too.' That was very important to him. He suddenly sat bolt upright. 'Do you think Maman would also like to have a picture from me?'

'I'm sure she would,' I concurred, ruffling his hair. 'But it shouldn't be so really, really big.'

'I know ... ' he giggled. 'Otherwise it won't fit in the coffer.'

I was momentarily dumbstruck by his choice of words – he had probably heard it on one of the treasure-hunter films that he loves to watch these days.

I glanced one last time at the 'painting' over his bed and shook my head, before turning off the light. I can only hope that Giulietta will 'go with him' for a very, very long time – otherwise we'll have to paint over the little girl Martian.

This is why you'll soon be receiving not only a letter from me, Hélène, but perhaps also a small artistic contribution from Arthur.

As I write this letter, the card I found in the 'coffer' on Friday is sitting in front of me.

I have read the quote from Tagore over and over again, but I still don't know what I should think of it. Which shut door am I staring at? Is that perhaps a reference to your grave? But what sense does that make when this door seems to somehow be permeable and open to me?

And then I have to wonder if any new doors have opened in my life. And who actually left the card for me? Was it you, my beloved Hélène?

On days like this, I tend to doubt that. And yet I so want to continue to chat together – you can see that I keep writing and telling you about my life without you, just like you made me promise.

When I was at your grave yesterday, Cathérine suddenly popped up, and she stared curiously at the card, which I was still holding. She claimed not to know the quote from Tagore, but could it really be coincidental that she appeared at the grave at that exact moment?

As we left the cemetery together, we ran into Sophie. The sculptor, remember? I told you about her. The two of them sized each other up like two tigresses, and later Cathérine asked rather sharply who that girl was who looked like a chimney sweep. How did we know each other?

When I explained that Sophie works at the cemetery, restoring and repairing the graves, her interest seemed to fade.

Women! They're all mysterious creatures. But not nearly as mysterious as the answers I've been getting to my letters. Where are these letters leading me, Hélène? Are they even leading me anywhere? Or are they simply a nice pastime, a kind of self-gratification for a man who has lost his wife and can't stop feeling sorry for himself, and thus clings to the last little trace of hope? Clings to a dead woman who is lost for ever? What kind of pointless game is that?

But what am I saying?! No, my love, forgive me! None of my letters to you are pointless, whether you are the one receiving them or someone else. I have so loved writing them.

And now I am standing here just like Orpheus, who wished so hard for his beloved Eurydice to return from the realm of shadows and who still ended up ultimately losing her. Because he doubted, because he looked back to see if the dear figure was actually following him, because he didn't hear any footsteps and didn't know if Eurydice was actually there.

I will never doubt that you're here, Hélène! I can't see you, but I know you exist.

I want to open all the shut doors and let in the light that you always were for me and perhaps still are.

Always
Julien

17

Orphée

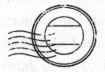

The following Saturday, I arrived completely out of breath at the small arthouse cinema on Rue Tholozé, which shows both contemporary and classic films. I was clutching my two tickets and was eager to know what was waiting for me here. I was a little late because I'd taken Arthur over to my mother's apartment, where he was going to spend the night. When we got there, we realised that he'd left Bruno at home. Arthur won't sleep anywhere without Bruno, so I had to run back to Rue Jacob to fetch his teddy bear.

The day before, when I was at the cemetery, I'd almost overlooked the two tickets. Not wanting to believe that the secret gravestone compartment was really empty, I looked closer and ran my fingers all around the cavity until I discovered the lavender pieces of paper that my envelope had inadvertently pushed against the back wall.

The tickets were for the Saturday evening show, reserved seats on the ninth row at Studio 28 on Montmartre. As if he had a sixth sense about such things, Alexandre called earlier in the day from his shop to see if I'd like to do something that evening. He wanted us to go out, and I said that I already had plans.

'Really? You have plans. What for?'

For a moment, I considered asking him to come with me to the theatre, but something stopped me. It was the thought of the mysterious stranger who might turn up at the cinema tonight to claim the second ticket. So I said that Cathérine had asked me to go to a film with her. Alexandre gave a long whistle and said he hoped I'd have a good time with Mademoiselle Balland.

Ironically, as Arthur and I were walking up Rue Bonaparte hand in hand, Cathérine appeared, heading toward us.

'Salut, you two,' she said in greeting. 'Are you off to do something fun?' Her eyes fell on the child-sized backpack I was carrying.

'I'm spending the night with Mamie.' Arthur smiled. 'She's making me cherry clafoutis.'

'That sounds delicious! Cherry clafoutis, mmmm ... I'm quite jealous. It's one of my favourites, too.'

Cathérine smiled questioningly at me, her pretty arched eyebrows lifting slightly. She had assumed her Julie Delpy look again. Groaning inside, I smiled back, but I had no desire to provide an explanation.

'Well, have a good evening, Cathérine. We need to hurry since my mother's expecting us,' I said in farewell.

I was sure she was still watching us in astonishment as we strode past the Deux Magots Café and crossed the Boulevard Saint-Germain.

I told my mother that I was going to the movies with Alexandre. She nodded happily, commenting that she was glad I was getting out a bit these days. This way, everyone was well and falsely informed.

By the time I dashed up the steps and into the small theatre, the other guests had already gone into the screening room. I cast my eyes around the lobby, hoping for the anonymous owner of the second ticket to materialise. The only person still in sight was an elderly gentleman standing a little irresolutely at the ticket counter.

I caught sight of the black-and-white poster in the display case, and my heart seemed to start pounding even faster than it had after jogging up the Montmartre Hill from the Metro station.

I stared mesmerised at the old photos of Jean Marais and Maria Casarès, and read the title of the film that was being shown this evening. It was Jean Cocteau's *Orphée*.

I quickly pushed my tickets toward the man sitting at the ticket counter. 'Is it too late for me to get in?'

'You're in luck, Monsieur. The film hasn't started yet.' He tore the tickets. 'Row nine – will someone be joining you?'

Was anyone else coming? I had been so hopeful, but it didn't look as if anybody was waiting for me. It could hardly be the old man who was standing around so uncertainly. I shook my head.

'No ... I ... I have one ticket too many. Feel free to give it to anyone who might like a seat.'

'Oh, I'd love to have the ticket,' the old man chimed in, who might have been old but was obviously not hard of hearing. 'All that are left are seats in the first two rows, but however much I love Cocteau, I hate getting a sore neck even more,' he explained to me as we walked into the darkened room and felt our way to our seats.

I murmured: 'Of course.'

I sat down in my seat, and was glad the film started only a few seconds later. The red curtain lifted as the noisy strains of melodramatic music began, sparing me any further conversation.

I admit that I was relatively speechless. In my last letter, I had described myself as Orpheus – and only a week later, I received tickets for the film *Orphée*.

I couldn't have asked for a stronger sign! I leaned back in my seat and breathlessly followed Cocteau's masterpiece, which I had never seen and which gave me more than one puzzling sentence to mull over.

The film was a retelling of the old myth of Orpheus and Eurydice. In this version, Orphée is a successful poet who has lost all of his inspiration and ideas. His rival, a young boozy fellow, who is accompanied by a stern princess dressed in black – apparently his patroness – is hanging around the Café des Poètes, the café favoured by poets, in a drunken haze and is hit by a car a short time later. The princess instructs her chauffeur to load the injured man into her black car and orders Orphée to come along as a witness.

While his pretty blonde wife, Eurydice, anxiously awaits his return, Orphée falls completely under the spell of the dark princess. At first he has no idea that she, Madame la Mort, is actually Death. The princess has designs on the poet, and she attempts to entice him with mystical sentences she is able to project through the car's radio. Orphée is fascinated, even obsessed, by these sentences, which sound like something from a surreal dream: 'A glass of water can illuminate the world' or 'Silence retreats more quickly – twice.' However, when the cruelly neglected Eurydice has an accident on her bicycle and dies, he decides to fetch her back from the underworld. With the help of the circumspect chauffeur Heurtebise – who is in reality a deceased student who had turned his gas on when his girlfriend left him – and a pair of special gloves, Orphée is able to pass through the bedroom mirror into the realm of the dead, where stricter laws apply than do on earth, and where there are no 'maybes'. Mirrors are the portals through which the dead can pass. Orphée is torn between his fascination with the Princess of Death and his pretty, naïve wife, who is expecting his child. He is allowed to take her out of the underworld, but is forbidden from ever looking at her. One day, their eyes meet by accident in the rearview mirror of a car, and Eurydice at once disappears. However, at the end of the film, Madame la Mort has a change of heart. She renounces love and, in order to grant the poet immortality, Orphée as well. She turns back time: 'Humans must be allowed to fulfil their fates.'

I lost myself in the film and its images, which exerted a unique fascination. It was as if the viewer were wandering through a strangely beautiful, rather spooky dream in the hope of seeing what was otherwise unseeable.

Was I a fanatic like Orphée? Who was my black princess, and who was Eurydice? Did I love death, or did I love life? I absorbed every image, every sentence, and when the red curtain lowered back over the screen, I woke up dazedly, as if from a deep sleep.

'It is still great art,' the old man next to me whispered approvingly as the lights went up. 'Thank you again for the ticket, young man.'

I nodded and stayed in my seat for a few more seconds.

As I stood up and glanced down the gradually emptying rows in front of me, I heard a silvery laugh.

I had to look twice to confirm that it was really her. There, two rows in front of me, stood a delicate girl in a white dress, chatting breezily with her friend. Her dark hair was loose and pulled back by a sparkling barrette.

I think it was the first time I'd seen Sophie wearing a dress. She looked exquisite. I had only seen her in overalls, and for a moment I stared admiringly at her as she laughed brightly once more.

Was that really Sophie?

At that moment, she turned her head a little to the side, and I recognised her heart-shaped face.

'Sophie?' I called quietly across the rows of seats. And then, louder: 'Sophie?'

She turned toward me, her face a single question.

'Julien?! What are you doing here? What a surprise!' she cried, and we worked our way down the row of seats until we could meet in the aisle.

'This is my cousin, Sabine.' She introduced her companion, who walked behind her like a queen, her ash-blonde hair pinned up and her posture perfect. Sophie shrugged. 'Sabine dragged me to this film, but I must admit it wasn't all that bad, was it?'

Sabine smiled regally, while Sophie's eyes slipped past me curiously. 'And who did you come with?'

'Oh, I'm here alone,' I said.

'Really?' she replied. 'Are you a big Cocteau fan?'

'It looks that way,' I said, laughing.

'Julien is also a writer,' she explained to her cousin, and shot me a smile. 'Although he always says he's just a lousy writer of light fiction.'

Sabine cocked her eyebrows, a gesture she seemed to have practised extensively. 'Truly entertaining people is an art that shouldn't be underestimated,' she declared, and I liked her right then and there. 'How about we get something to drink? The theatre has a nice outdoor bar. If we hurry, we can get seats.'

'Good idea!' Sophie exclaimed, immediately rummaging around for something in her small handbag. 'Go on. I'll just call and say I'll be out longer.'

A few minutes later we were sitting in a tiny courtyard located next to the café inside the theatre. Round Moroccan tables and potted palms had transformed this spot into an oasis. Black-and-white photos of famous actors were pasted together to create a gigantic collage. I recognised Jean-Louis Barrault, the melancholy mime from *Children of Paradise*, Brigitte Bardot, Jeanne Moreau, Cathérine Deneuve, Marlon Brando and Humphrey Bogart in his unmistakable Philip Marlowe trench coat. Every table in the small café was taken, and with our wine in hand we were happy to be among the select few who had managed to get a place here on this pleasant evening. We started out talking about the film, and then moved on to all sorts of other topics. Sophie was tactful enough to not mention that we knew each other from the cemetery.

For a change, the fact that I had lost my wife and was a widower didn't matter one single bit this evening. Sabine had serious, intelligent eyes, but she could also be very funny. She worked as a culture editor for a magazine, and knew all sorts of insider stuff about books and films, which she voiced in vivid terms. She even knew my first novel, which she'd found 'extremely amusing'. For some reason, this cheered me up.

The evening flew by. We didn't notice that the small courtyard was empty until the waiter started to rather noisily shove the chairs under the tables.

Sophie glanced at her watch.

'*Mon Dieu!* It's past one o'clock,' she exclaimed, turning to the waiter with a winsome smile. 'Thank you for putting up with us so long.'

I insisted on paying for the wine – after all, I had received the tickets for free – and we said goodbye at the bottom of the theatre steps.

'It was nice to meet you, Julien,' Sabine said, handing me her card. 'If you ever start doubting that you can write, just give me a call. I'd be glad to tell you how good you are.' Her mouth curled into a mocking smile, and her eyes twinkled – an echo of Sophie.

I stuck the card in my pocket and nodded. 'I'll keep that in mind.'

'Take care, Sophie. See you soon! Tell *Chouchou* hello for me.' Sabine kissed her cousin on both cheeks and then walked down the street, her cape swirling around her.

Sophie grinned. 'That was Sabine,' she remarked. 'My favourite cousin.' She cocked her head to one side and smiled. 'I have no cards with me, author, but it would be just fine if you wanted to call me in case you ever need someone to tell you how wonderful you really are.' She winked. 'I'd be glad to give you my cell number.'

'That's not necessary,' I said, also smiling.

Sophie pulled a shawl around her shoulders and looked up into the sky, where the moon floated, full and silent.

'It's so quiet at this hour,' she commented. 'I think I like Montmartre the best at night.' She looked at me. 'Want to walk a little?'

We strolled down the street together.

'That was a really strange film . . . strange and beautiful at the same time,' she said.

I nodded vaguely as she absentmindedly climbed the steps to Place Émile Goudeau, which sat under its tall trees, silent and enchanted. The small restaurant on the lower side of the square had shut its doors hours ago, and closed white parasols stood between the empty chairs, like sentinels of the night.

Slowing her pace, Sophie paused beside the old-fashioned water fountain in the middle of the square, inside its ring of four greenish shimmering caryatids.

'I liked one particular sentence a lot.'

'Which sentence do you mean?'

Her face turned dreamy. 'Every world is touched by love.'

'Yes, that is a very lovely sentence.'

'Do you think there are other worlds besides our own, Julien?'

'Perhaps. It sometimes seems that way, doesn't it? The universe is so unbelievably large.'

'Unending,' she said. 'That's practically impossible for us to comprehend.'

Our footsteps echoed off the pavement.

'You know what? That man, Orphée, reminded me a little of you.'

'Why? Because of his dead wife?'

'No, because he almost picked the wrong side.' She smiled. 'In any case, I'm very glad the black princess released Orphée. Life should always win in the end, not death.'

We stopped walking and looked at each other. For a moment, it felt like our hearts touched across the few steps that separated our bodies.

'This is where we part ways,' she then said. 'I have to go along here, and you have to head down there. Good night, Julien!'

'Good night, Sophie,' I replied.

I watched her go. An impish wind was playing with the hem of her dress, and with sudden regret, it occurred to me that the nicest girls were always taken.

18

The map of my heart

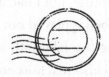

I had a growing feeling that I was caught inside a film. I kept thinking about my evening at the theatre, and the swirl of images in my head churned up a stream of other images. And then I found the map.

It happened on a hot July day around noon, an hour when the cemetery was typically deserted. Sophie was also nowhere to be seen. As I opened the compartment to drop off my latest letter, I discovered a map of Paris, which was obviously far from new. I glanced all around before sticking it in my satchel.

Seriously? I thought. Why would a Parisian need a map of Paris?

'Is this some kind of joke?' I grumbled quietly, gazing at the bronze head whose neutral smile didn't flicker. 'Oh well, I guess no answer is a kind of answer.'

I stepped behind the gravestone to pull out the vase that sat there, then filled it with water from a nearby tap and eased my bouquet inside it.

I had accomplished quite a bit since that evening at the theatre. Like a man possessed, I had written fifty new pages – real, authentic pages that had more in common with my life than the plot I'd invented for the other book which had unexpectedly won the Prix Goncourt. And when Jean-Pierre Favre asked me over lunch at Le Petit Zinc how everything was going, I stared at the lovely Art Nouveau woman standing behind him on her pedestal, sniffing her flowers, and answered enthusiastically that my novel would be finished by the end of the year. I admit that prediction was a little premature, but I had a strong feeling that by that point, the invisible thread being played out by my mysterious Ariadne would lead me back out of the labyrinth of my life. And when that happened, my novel would also reach its conclusion.

Luckily, we didn't discuss the book's content, otherwise Monsieur Favre would have choked on his steak tartare with its raw egg garnish.

'Marvellous!' he cried as he cheerfully forked a portion into his mouth. I wasn't sure if his enthusiasm was inspired by the raw beef or by the fact that his author had obviously rediscovered his rhythm.

Besides that, I had actually made plans for the summer holiday. At first, I failed to realise that the nursery school was going to close for a few weeks during the summer. That's how much I was caught up in my own little film. Cathérine was actually the one who reminded me about the holiday one afternoon when I picked Arthur up from her apartment.

'Do you have plans for the summer break?' she asked, and for a moment I stared at her cluelessly.

'Hmm ... Well ...' I snatched at the first idea that came to me. 'I think we'll go to Honfleur. But thanks for saying something. I need to discuss the details with my mother.'

Arthur looked up from the picture book he had just been paging through.

'Can Giulietta come, too?' he asked. 'That would be so cool, Papa!'

I was struck by the sudden vision of the two children decorating the entire house in Honfleur with fingerpaint, and I had to sigh as I smiled: 'I think that might be a little too much for Mamie.'

Arthur shook his head. 'Mamie already said Giulietta could come,' he declared.

'What?' I was caught by surprise. 'You already asked Mamie?'

Cathérine chuckled when she saw my astonishment. 'It looks as if your son plans a little further in advance than you do, Julien. He definitely gets that from Hélène. Remember how much she loved to make plans?'

We both laughed – we had reached the point of being able to talk about Hélène's endearing quirks without getting melancholy. For a moment, I recalled all those New Year's days on which Hélène could think of no nicer activity than to sit down at the table and fill out her new calendar: birthdays, concerts, weekends with friends or relatives, nursery-school activities, day trips, vacations.

'Writing down the joys,' she had always called it.

And so I spoke with Maman and then with Giulietta's parents. Eventually the plan was for Maman to travel to the coast in August for two weeks with Camille, Aunt Carole's daughter, and the two children. I intended to join them at the end of that time for another two weeks, allowing Camille to return to Paris with Giulietta. It had been a long time since I'd been to Honfleur, and I was looking forward to seeing the old house where I had spent so many wonderful summers as a child.

That was the plan.

But we plan, and God laughs.

As I strolled down the cemetery path that afternoon, sunk in my thoughts, I had no idea that I wouldn't be going to Honfleur this summer. There was much I had no idea about at that point. Looking back, it seems as if I was utterly blind.

I walked down Avenue Hector Berlioz. As so often before, the grim caretaker trudged toward me, dragging behind him a grey garbage sack, this time stuffed with plant debris. He glared at me in silence. And then I noticed a large black hat bobbing among some bushes behind a gravestone. It belonged to a lady in an elegant black outfit who was standing in front of a grave watched over by a tall stone angel. Of course, I couldn't help thinking about Alexandre's theory about the lovely widow and Sophie's comment about catching sight several times of a woman in a large hat around the cemetery. However, the lady wasn't standing at Hélène's grave. As for me, I had more important things to do than shadow widows in black. Besides, I was getting hungry.

I ate at a Moroccan restaurant on the Boulevard de Clichy. While I waited for my lamb tagine with couscous, I pulled the map of Paris that I'd found in the gravestone out of my bag, unfolded it awkwardly on the loaded table, and examined the snarl of alleys, streets and wide boulevards. As I've said, it wasn't a new map, and it was ripped at several spots.

As I scanned the map, I discovered that a circle had been drawn in ink around a small square. To the right of it was a star, the kind used for footnotes.

Strange.

I leaned closer and realised that what had been marked was Jehan

Rictus Square – a small square very close to the Abbesses Metro station and not far from the bistro in which I was currently sitting. What was located there?

My tagine arrived, and the scent of braised lamb, dates and honey filled my nose. I was quickly and rather ineptly refolding the map – I'm clumsy with such things – when I realised that someone had written something on the reverse side of the map. The sentence was marked with another star:

When in love, a person tosses their heart over the wall and jumps after it.

Nobody had ever wolfed down tagine as rapidly as I then did, doing a grave disservice to the marvellous dish that had spent hours braising in the oven until the tender meat fell off the bone as soon as the fork touched it.

I swallowed several scrumptious bites, took one large gulp of red wine, and called for my cheque.

The dark-skinned waiter looked at me as if I had personally insulted him.

'You didn't enjoy it, Monsieur?'

'Not at all! It was wonderful.' I stood up hastily, almost tipping over the chair. 'I've just found out I have to go, that's all.' I glanced quickly at the map to figure out the shortest route to Jehan Rictus Square.

The waiter nodded concernedly. He had no idea what was wrong. Anyone who left such good lamb tagine on his plate couldn't be from anywhere around here.

'Can I help you, Monsieur? Do you know where you're going?'

'Of course I do. I'm from Paris.'

I stuffed the map into my satchel and set off.

*

A few minutes later, my heart pounding loudly, I was standing at Jehan Rictus Square. It was a small, shady square, one side of it enclosed by an inscribed wall. I had heard about this wall (since, after all, I grew up here in Paris), but had never seen it personally. It was the famous *mur des je t'aime* – an old house wall on which was mounted a gigantic panel displaying the phrase that has always made our world turn round, supposedly written in every language that exists.

I love you.

I love you – hundreds, thousands of times.

I had no idea who had thrown their heart over the wall. Map in hand, I sank down on a nearby bench which commanded a good view of the *mur des je t'aime*.

I learned much about love that afternoon.

I saw two friends standing arm in arm by the wall as they read aloud the various sentences. I saw lovers gaze into each other's eyes and kiss. I watched as newlyweds had themselves photographed in front of the wall, so they could later share this moment with their children. I saw two Brits take pictures of each other jumping across the face of the wall. I saw a group of Japanese tourists tirelessly wave and laugh and form hearts with their hands. I saw a girl carrying a backpack stand motionlessly beside the wall for a long time. And an elderly couple, awkwardly holding hands, grateful that life had granted them such a long time together.

I observed so many people that day – people of every age and from every country imaginable. However, they all had one thing in common: when they turned and walked away, every one of them wore a smile.

The afternoon sun was setting swiftly by the time I abandoned my seat on the bench. As I stood up I heard a sharp 'ping' emanate from my bag. I pulled out my phone and found a text message from Alexandre, who had obviously been trying all afternoon to reach me. I gazed at the screen and had to grin.

So where are you hiding? Heading off again somewhere with the pretty neighbour? You can't fool me, my friend.

Alexandre just couldn't let it go. Ever since the two of us had allegedly gone to the movies together, he simply didn't want to believe that there was nothing going on between Cathérine and me.

I dialled his number, and he picked up immediately.

'Good grief, Julien, where have you been all day? You're harder to reach than the Pope,' he grumbled. 'Cellphones are great things, but you actually have to check them.'

'Now I'm here, what's so important?' I asked, amused.

I glanced once more at the wall where a young woman with flaming red hair was now standing, studying the inscriptions across the plaque. She slowly turned around, and for a moment, I thought I was staring at Hélène. As she finished her rotation, everything around me seemed to come to a stop.

'Alexandre, I have to go,' I rasped into the phone.

Only a few metres away from me stood Caroline – the same Caroline with whom I had chatted about Jacques Prévert's poems on the steps of the Sacré-Cœur – and she was smiling at me.

Hélène, my beloved,
    It is late already. Arthur is fast asleep in his room,
and I'm sitting at my desk, still wound up by all that has
happened today.

When I dropped off my letter for you, I discovered a map of Paris in the secret compartment. Thanks to a circled spot and a charming sentence about walls and hearts, this map led me to le mur des je t'aime.

I sat on a bench there for an age, watching the people who came to the Wall of Love, and oddly moved by the scenes that played themselves out. I sat, watched and waited, until suddenly I was overcome by the desire to once again be able to say: 'I love you' to someone who could gaze at me and take my hand the way you used to, Hélène.

I had to call Alexandre back at one point, and for a moment I was distracted. But then I looked up and saw YOU standing there next to the wall, Hélène. For a second, my heart literally stopped, and I felt like I was in free fall.

But it was actually Caroline, the red-haired student from the Sacré-Cœur. Remember her? The one who likes to read poetry and who reminded me of you, mon amour, that other time? The young woman who spoke to me on the day I found the stone heart, that first sign. And once again, my dumb heart began to stumble.

Caroline stood there as if she were the answer to all my questions. She smiled at me, and I was suddenly absolutely certain that she was the one who had left me all the clues and who had finally led me to this wall.

I staggered toward her.

'Caroline,' I exclaimed. 'Caroline! Was it you? Did you leave all those signs for me?'

Her eyes were friendly, but also confused.

'Which signs?' she asked, baffled. 'What do you mean, Monsieur?'

'But ... but ... what are you doing here?' I stammered. 'Why are you here right now, at this wall of all places?'

'Well,' she said with a slightly embarrassed laugh. 'I wanted to see the famous mur des je t'aime and ... take a picture.' She brushed back her red hair. 'Oh, this is embarrassing. You must think I plan to take selfies in front of all of Paris's landmarks, just like any silly tourist.'

She giggled, but broke off in surprise when she saw all the colour drain from my face. 'Are you feeling sick, Monsieur? Let's go sit down.'

She took my arm and guided me back to the bench I'd just come from. I leaned forward and rested my head in my hands as I tried to pull myself together. What in the world had I been thinking? I was losing it – this student who was spending a semester in Paris didn't even know my name, much less anything about the grave!

The embarrassment was wholly mine.

'Pardon me. For a second, I mistook you for ... someone else,' I explained, glancing up. 'And then everything started spinning around me.'

Caroline nodded. 'Circulation. I know what that's like. Maybe you've been in the sun too long.' She rummaged around in her leather backpack. 'Here, take this, Monsieur. I always carry a sugar cube with me for when that happens.'

She held out a wrapped sugar cube covered in paper decorated with green writing. I slowly unwrapped it and stuck it in my mouth. The sugar crunched between my teeth as I cautiously chewed on it.

'And . . . feel any better?' Caroline watched me anxiously.

If she thought I was some kind of freak who just sat around staring at walls and making strange remarks, she didn't let on.

'Yes . . . thank you.' My faintness passed. I looked at the sugar wrapper and had to smile. 'I see you've already been to Café de Flore. You really are making your way around,' I said lightly, attempting to guide our conversation back into normal waters.

She grinned. 'I'm doing research for my bachelor's thesis. I have to visit all the places Prévert and his Groupe Octobre went.'

We stayed on the bench for a few more minutes, and Caroline told me about her research. I admit I only understood about half of what she was saying, but that might have been due to the fact that I was exhausted. Exhausted by the unsettling things that were going on in my real life, as well as by the things that merely existed in my imagination.

She eventually stood up and held out her phone to me.

'Would you mind taking another photo of me – or better yet, a short video of me in front of the wall?' She straightened her cardigan, smoothing it over her summery dress.

The video was for her boyfriend Michael, who had already returned to London. He was missing her terribly, she explained with a wink. She showed me which button to hit in order to record the video, and then asked:

'What's your name, Monsieur – in case we run into each other again?'

'Azoulay,' I said. 'Julien Azoulay.'

'All right, Monsieur Azoulay, let's get started,' she called. 'But you have to get the wall in the picture.'

I nodded, raised the phone and tapped the button.

Caroline walked over to the wall, stood facing it for a moment, and then slowly turned around. A smile spread across her face, one that was so young, so gloriously young. She held her arms out as if she wanted to embrace the entire world and cried:

'Je t'aime!!!'

Oh, Hélène! We used to be like that – so happy and carefree and younger than a day in May. What would I have given for those words to have been meant for me? I miss you so much, mon amour, but I also miss having love in my life. Yes, I so want to be happy again, Hélène. I think of you as a lovely dream. Why couldn't you have been the one standing in front of the wall and calling 'I love you!!!'?

I have already written you so many letters. There aren't many more to go until I reach the thirty-third. I both long to reach that final letter, and also fear it.

What will happen once I've written that letter, Hélène? What will happen? Will you suddenly be standing there waiting for me? Will someone be standing there? Or no one?

I don't know, I don't know anything any more. All I know is that I can't take this game much longer. I've started to see ghosts, and in my confusion I've begun to accost total strangers. This can't continue, it must end.

Oh, my beloved angel, I'm in such a mess.

What should I do, my soulmate? You were always that for me and still are – the woman at my side who never failed to cheer me up whenever I despaired. That was so important to me, and always helped.

But now I need a glimmer of hope, Hélène. I need that desperately! I will hold out my arms and wait.

Come into my night and bring your light!
Julien

P.S. I had already stuck this letter in an envelope by the time I remembered something. Arthur painted a picture for you, which I was ordered to put in the 'coffer'. Here it is. Since learning to write his name, he signs all his pictures with 'ATUR'. He asked me this evening if I thought you would like the picture, and I told him I knew that you were sure to. THAT I know without a doubt.

19

Discoveries

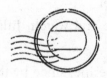

'Know what, my friend? I have a feeling that someone's been playing you. And I happen to know who it is, too.'

I was sitting with Alexandre in a café on Rue de Grenelle, not far from L'espace des rêveurs. We'd taken a small streetside table, and the ashtray next to me was almost full.

As a result of my abruptly hanging up on him after catching sight of Caroline at the Wall of Love, Alexandre had threatened to terminate our friendship if I didn't *instantly* come to him and explain what the hell was going on.

But *instantly* wasn't possible from my end, since I had to pick up Arthur from nursery school. Besides that, I wanted time to organise my thoughts, which didn't turn out to be a very successful effort. This was why I trudged over to Rue de Grenelle with mixed feelings the following day at noon, where I faced Alexandre's intrusive questions and told him everything. He managed to refrain from making any remarks about unhappy, unstable widowers.

'Man,' was all he said, 'that's quite the story.' He grinned. 'Just wait until everyone at my club hears about this.'

'Which club?' I asked. 'The Dead Poets Society?'

'Haha,' Alexandre chuckled. 'Still a shred left of your famous wit.'

He beckoned the waiter and ordered two servings of *steak frites*. 'Don't protest,' he said. 'And take this with you, *s'il vous plaît*.' He held out the ashtray to the waiter.

'You need to hide there and watch, Julien,' Alexandre continued. 'Then you'll catch her.'

By 'her', he meant Cathérine, since by this point no one else came into question for him. It was either her or a random psychopath about whom we knew nothing, and how likely was that?

'She's the one, Julien. One hundred per cent. Excuse me for being so blunt, but she's the only one who's interested in you. I don't see any other options.' He took a sip of wine, doing his best Sherlock Holmes. 'You have to figure out the motive.'

I shook my head. 'You're way off the mark, believe me.'

'Shush, Watson. Why haven't you just asked her? Outright?'

'Because I have no desire to make a fool of myself again, which is what would happen. I'd ask her why she's taken my letters, and she'd look at me like I'd grown a third eye.' The thought of sharing more of myself with Cathérine for no compelling reason made me quite uncomfortable.

'I know Cathérine,' I declared like an idiot. 'She wouldn't do anything like that.'

'But why are you so defensive about this possibility? Your neighbour has a motive, plus she was your wife's friend, plus she knows your routine. I bet Cathérine knows exactly on which days you go to the cemetery.'

I recalled our interactions in the lobby. Cathérine saying: *Well, Julien, heading to Montmartre?* And me answering: *I like to make myself scarce on Fridays when Louise is tearing through the apartment.*

'Others know that, too,' I said.

'Really? Who?'

'For example, my mother.'

'Come on. Don't give me that with your mother. That's ridiculous.'

'Hmm,' I replied. I wasn't convinced. 'And what do you really have in mind? Should I set up a one-man tent in the cemetery and keep the grave under surveillance?'

Alexandre looked thoughtful for a moment.

'You could at least change your routine,' he suggested.

As a result, I decided to head to Montmartre on Wednesday this week, admittedly with no great hope of obtaining any new insights. Nonetheless, since Alexandre had insisted on this minor change, I followed through on it, if only to be able to tell him that going on another day hadn't made a difference.

This didn't turn out to be so.

I had just stepped through the gates of the Cimetière Montmartre, letter and flowers in hand, when I heard someone call my name.

It was Sophie, who was perched on top of the cemetery wall like the first time I saw her. I waved briefly and left the Avenue Hector Berlioz to cross over to her, weaving between the gravestones.

'Why the grim face, author?' I felt dizzy just watching her sway back and forth. 'Even at a hundred metres away, anyone could tell that you're in a bad mood.'

'Be careful, or you'll fall off,' I said. Good grief, I really was in a foul mood. 'How are you doing?' I added. I hadn't seen Sophie since the night at the movies.

She shifted her position and stretched out like Goethe in the Roman Campagna: on her side, leg bent and arm draped casually over her knee. She studied me pensively.

'Not all that amazing either, but obviously better than you,' she declared.

'Oh! Relationship woes?' I asked.

'Who knows?' she answered with a grin. 'I've been thinking a lot about that evening at the theatre. And about Orpheus. You, too?'

'Honestly – no,' I confessed. At the moment, I seemed to be going from one emotional extreme to the next.

'Pity,' she said, sitting back up.

As I watched her scoot around the wall, the sentence from the map suddenly came to me.

'I have a nice sentence for you, though.'

'Now you've got me curious,' she said. 'Spit it out!'

'When in love, a person tosses their heart over the wall and jumps after it.'

She cocked her head and considered the sentiment for a moment.

'That really is a nice sentence,' she replied. 'Did you write it?'

'No.' I shook my head as my eyes caught hers.

For a moment, neither of us said anything.

'Who did?' she finally asked.

'No idea. I thought you might be able to tell me.'

She wrinkled her brow and shook her head. 'I'm afraid I can't help you, author,' she said. 'However, it's a nice, true sentence. When you love someone, you shouldn't spend too much time analysing it.' She tugged her cap lower over her forehead and looked at the flowers I was holding. 'Heading to the grave?'

I nodded.

'Want to go get something to drink afterward? I'll be done in just a minute, and it's such a pretty day.'

She smiled at me, and I nodded, sensing that my mood was brightening.

'Sounds great. I'll be right back and pick you up.'

'*Très bien*,' Sophie said. 'See you in a bit, Julien.'

She turned back to her tools which were spread out beside her atop the wall, and I made my way back to the main path.

A few minutes later, I was slipping my letter into Hélène's gravestone. This time I found a square envelope inside the cavity. A silver disk was tucked inside – either a CD or a DVD, but without any writing on it. Surprised, I stuck it in my small brown leather bag and shut the compartment. I stood back up and glanced around the lush verdant landscape. At the other end of the cemetery I noticed a small figure heading toward me from the entrance along the Avenue Hector Berlioz.

I felt foolish as I retreated a few metres and hid behind another gravestone. Alexandre's advice to watch and wait shot through my mind, and I choked back a hysterical laugh. I stood motionlessly behind the random gravestone and waited in vain, like Samuel Beckett's hero.

Whoever was coming up the avenue wouldn't take the small path to the old chestnut tree and stop at Hélène's grave.

I was wrong about that.

*

After a few minutes, which felt like an eternity, I heard footsteps cautiously draw closer. Someone stepped past the angel, leaned down, pushed the marble plaque aside, and extracted an envelope.

My heart raced, as I peered around the edge of the gravestone. It only took one glance for me to recognise the woman who hastily opened my letter and began to read it.

It was Cathérine!

I can't even describe what shot through me at that moment. My emotions were too fragmented. A combination of anger, astonishment and profound disappointment bubbled up to the surface.

It actually was Cathérine! Of all people!

Alexandre had been right. Blithering Cathérine with her guileless blue eyes! I think I would have preferred to see anyone else in the world at Hélène's grave than my blonde neighbour. Even a widow in a black hat would have been better. How hypocritical! I lost control as my anger blew up.

'Aha! I caught you!' I leaped out from behind the gravestone as I yelled this, and Cathérine gave a startled cry. She dropped the letter, and Arthur's picture sailed across the path like a giant leaf.

'Julien!' Her wide eyes stared at me. 'What are you doing here?'

I stood right in front of her. 'What am *I* doing here?' I yelled. She flinched at each question as if I were whipping her. 'What are *you* doing here?! You're creeping around the grave and stealing my letters! *Reading* my letters. I can't believe this! They're private, understand? Private! How could you do this?'

As her eyes filled with tears, she gazed at me contritely. I felt a strong urge to shake her.

'Stop blubbering! You're just making it worse!' I was beside myself. 'Of all the dishonest behaviours! I felt like I was losing my mind, doubted my own sanity. And Mademoiselle here has been helping herself to one letter after the other, leaving little tokens behind to soften me up.'

'Julien . . . I . . . I don't know . . .' she stammered as the colour drained from her face.

'And what?!' I hurled at her. 'YOU read all of them. You know my thoughts, my hopes, my stupid ideas. You took all my letters, leaving things behind for me in the gravestone – poems, music boxes, maps, cards with quotes from Tagore . . . I convinced myself that I was communicating with a dead person while all the time you're the . . . YOU! I can't believe it!' I spun around, ready to stomp off in fury.

Cathérine began to cry in earnest. 'Julien, Julien!' she sobbed. 'No, please don't go. At least, hear what I have to say.'

'No way. I've seen enough. I'm done letting myself be led down the garden path.'

She clutched my arm. 'Please, Julien! I understand that you're horribly upset, but I didn't lead you on. I never left anything in that compartment, no music boxes or maps. And as for this letter here' – she gestured at the pages that were scattered around the path – 'it was the first and only one I've read.'

I stopped and stared at her in astonishment.

'You want me to believe that?'

'Please, Julien! This really was the only letter,' she insisted, wringing her hands nervously. 'I swear it on . . . on . . . Arthur's life,' she stammered as tears trickled down her cheeks. 'I didn't know anything about the compartment in the gravestone.'

'Then how do you know about it now?'

She wiped away her tears. 'Arthur ... Arthur told me about it last week ... when he was painting that picture for Hélène. He told me that you sometimes take letters to the cemetery and that there was a secret compartment in the gravestone where you stick them. "But it's a secret," he told me. "Not even Sophie knows about it." And then he suddenly told me about the nice woman from the cemetery who repairs angels. He also said you like her a lot and laugh with her. I was jealous, just like that.' She hiccuped.

'Good grief, Cathérine!'

'Please forgive me, Julien. You have to forgive me,' she pleaded. 'I'm not a bad person. I ... I just wanted to know ... I mean ... I thought maybe you'd written something about you and Sophie in this letter ...' She hung her head. 'It was a huge mistake, Julien. Please don't stay angry with me.'

I sank down numbly onto the small wall that surrounded the grave. 'I can't believe this is happening.'

Cathérine joined me on the wall. For a while, we sat there in silence, staring at the small path. From somewhere came a little sneeze. Or it might have been a cat hissing or a bird fussing among the chestnut leaves.

As if at a secret signal, Cathérine turned toward me and clasped my hand.

'I really didn't take any other letters except this one, Julien,' she declared. 'Please believe me!'

I stared at her. A liar didn't look like this.

'All right. I believe you, Cathérine.'

'And – you forgive me, too?'

I nodded slowly.

'Thank you.'

I stood up, and Cathérine also rose to her feet. She hesitated.

'Do you think . . . that someday there might . . . be something between us?'

'Oh, Cathérine!' I pressed my lips together and shook my head. 'To be honest, I don't think so, but what do I know? I'm just human.'

'And . . . and what's going on between you and this Sophie right now?'

'What are you talking about?' I said, annoyed, as I brushed the dirt off my pants.

'I mean . . . are you in love with her?' she asked shyly.

Her questions were getting out of line.

'Cathérine, stop right now,' I insisted, louder than necessary. 'Sophie is just a random acquaintance from the cemetery, that's all. I loved Hélène, I loved her very much. I still love her, if you really must know. And I have no idea if I can ever love another woman,' I added defiantly. 'Is that clear enough for you?'

She nodded meekly. 'Yes, Julien.'

She gathered up the pages of my letter from the ground, and handed them to me along with Arthur's picture and the envelope.

'I should leave now.' Shoulders slumped, she trudged off down the winding path.

I stood at Hélène's grave for several minutes, gazing blankly at my lovely angel. I can't claim that I was doing well at that moment.

Alexandre's theory had been right after all. And at the same time, he'd been wrong. Cathérine was interested in me, more than I'd thought she was, more than I'd wanted to admit. But she hadn't taken the letters. She didn't have anything to do with all the little gifts left for me.

Or did she?

My head began to buzz like a swarm of bees.

If she hadn't done it, then who had?

Oh, Hélène, what an almighty mess!

I stuck the letter back in its envelope and set it inside the compartment, which was still standing open. As I walked down the cemetery paths, I felt as sluggish as an old man.

It wasn't until the subway doors hissed shut behind me that I remembered I was supposed to meet Sophie. I stared into the darkness of the tunnel as we raced into it, little suspecting that it would be a long time until I saw the sculptor again.

20

The long silence

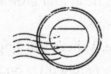

Sometimes so much happens in such a short time span, and events pile on top of each other and take your breath away. And at other times, nothing happens for weeks on end.

I had entered the second of these phases.

Silence reigned – silence from all sides. And this silence was getting to me.

Cathérine was avoiding me. After the confrontation in the cemetery, the invitations to her apartment stopped, and when Arthur went to her place to play, she always dropped him off at our apartment door and departed quickly. Whenever we ran into each other in the hall, she slipped past me with a murmured *Bonjour* and lowered eyes. She was ashamed. My harsh words might have hurt her. She retreated, and I wouldn't have been surprised, if looking back, she had felt offended by me. Cathérine was just the type to wrap herself in silence in such a situation, even though it was she who had taken my letter and set off my reaction. Oh well, perhaps I had reacted too intensely, but at any rate I had forgiven her in the end. There was no call for her to play the injured party here.

The sculptor also seemed to have vanished into thin air. Over the next few weeks, every time I went to the cemetery I watched out for her. No, I actually searched for her everywhere. I even asked the glum caretaker if he had seen the conservator, or if her tool bag was in the shed. But the caretaker just shook his head and growled morosely that the stone breaker didn't come any more.

This was all very strange. Where was Sophie? Now that I could no longer assume that she was perched up on some wall and calling out to me, or somewhere around to chat with, I began to miss her. I felt guilty whenever I thought about how I had described her as a 'random acquaintance' in my fury at Cathérine. And now I missed her – her one-off comments, her advice, her proverbs, her large, dark eyes as they peered out from under her cap. The way she would teasingly ask me: 'Why the grim face, author?!' That especially.

Had she fallen sick? Had her work at the Cimetière Montmartre somehow come to an end? She wouldn't have just up and disappeared without telling me, would she?

At first, I didn't feel her absence all that acutely, and I didn't think anything of it. She had sometimes gone missing before for a few days at a time, but then the small black figure would pop up somewhere out of the bushes to chip away at one gravestone or the other, to sit up in trees or on benches, and cheer me up with her insights and good spirits.

On that disastrous Wednesday – before I discovered Cathérine at the grave and raged so badly that I yelled like a lunatic in the cemetery and then forgot to meet Sophie – everything had been like normal. She had sat on the wall and joked with me a little, as she always did – not a word about her work at the cemetery coming to an end. And I couldn't imagine that she'd been offended when I didn't come by to take her out for a drink afterwards. It had been a casual date of sorts, and it wouldn't have been like Sophie to retreat into her snail shell the way Cathérine was doing at the moment.

On Friday, two days after the incident, I went back to the cemetery to offer Sophie some kind of excuse for why I'd bailed on her on Wednesday, as well as a casual apology. I had decided to invite her out for lunch to make amends. I didn't bring a letter on this particular day. I had lost my eagerness to write them, at least for now, and I didn't go by the grave. I really only went to find Sophie.

But she wasn't there. Not on that day, or any that followed. Three weeks passed by without a trace.

I kept thinking about our last encounter. She had accused me of being in a bad mood – a true assessment at that – although my mood had been fantastic when compared with what later happened at Hélène's grave. Sophie had lolled around on top of the wall like a cat in a sunbeam, but – and this only struck me later, when I carefully reviewed the words we had exchanged – hadn't she also said that although she was doing better than me, she wasn't doing so great?

And what if she really was having relationship problems? She might have told me about them that day, and I would have been in a position to help console her for a change. Maybe that Chouchou had dumped her, and she was curled up with a broken heart, weeping, somewhere in her small attic apartment in Montmartre.

It wasn't like I knew exactly where Sophie lived. Or with whom. After the film, we had walked around a little, and then she had stopped at a fork in the street and sent me off.

I wished I could have just called her. I groaned as I once again remembered how nonchalantly I had brushed off her phone number. 'No need,' I'd said. '*No need.*'

What a blind idiot I'd been!

I must have searched for her cousin's business card at least a hundred times. That evening I had carelessly stuck it somewhere. Now I couldn't find it, and couldn't recall the editor's full name, which would at least have helped some.

I had even searched online for *Sophie Claudel, sculptor*, but that hadn't turned up anything useful either.

When I considered everything closely – something I had plenty of time to do during those long weeks – I realised that I actually knew next to nothing about Sophie. Almost all of our conversations had focused on me. On my unhappiness, my mourning, my writer's block, my inability to cope with the things in my life. For the first time, I recognised that in my pain, I had only ever concentrated on myself. There had been only me, then nothing at all for a long time. And yet Sophie had kept reaching out to me, kept trying to figure things out, to advise and cheer me up. The heart of the stone worker with the large dark eyes was actually as soft as butter. And yet she could also tease and act brusquely at times. What else could have motivated her to care so much about my emotional well-being? To ask about my little boy? To get so involved in my life story?

Sophie had everything. She was young, she was pretty. She had a job she loved, and a boyfriend. At least, she had had him as long as I'd known her. Everything else was speculation. She was rash, eccentric and impulsive. And she was just the kind of girl to throw her heart over a wall and jump after it if she cared for someone.

All of a sudden, I thought of a thousand things I wanted to ask her about, but Sophie remained missing.

On the other hand, my letter – the last one I'd brought to the grave before Cathérine removed it from the secret compartment – was still sitting in the gravestone.

Each time I went to the cemetery, I checked on the opened envelope which I had returned to the compartment after the incident. Nobody had moved it since then. The letter marked with the number 31 sat in the small cavity like a silent reproach. One week, two weeks, three weeks.

There were also no more signs. I had obviously drawn the fury of all women onto myself. Nobody spoke to me any more. Nobody called out for me, nobody left me any messages. And after a while, I felt like that even Hélène had abandoned me. I was too disappointed to draw the right conclusions. Instead I wondered what I had done to dissolve the magic.

Worst of all, I had also lost my little leather bag with the silver disk in it on that galling day when I caught Cathérine red-handed. I was convinced that the little disk could have given me the explanation to everything, but it seemed that it was gone.

The fact that the whole game ended the moment I surprised Cathérine at the grave was naturally telling. Could it really be a coincidence? Not according to Alexandre. For him, the case was very clear cut.

'Damn your gut feelings,' he said in his gruff fashion, as I was once again overcome by doubt. 'Of course, Cathérine didn't tell you the whole truth. I bet that all your letters are sitting in her nightstand.'

'No, Alexandre, I simply don't agree,' I'd said, recalling how Cathérine had sworn on my son's life that she was innocent of that. 'I don't think she did it.'

'You've been wrong about Cathérine already. The fact is that you caught her, and since then, nobody has shown any interest in your letters, not even Hélène. What could be more obvious? I mean, how blind can you be?'

Maybe I really was struck blind during those weeks. Sometimes you need a little more time to comprehend the things your heart has known for ages.

And yet, the ending was different than Alexandre thought.

Completely different.

August descended. Paris seemed to be empty, and only a few tourists were left to wander around the hot pavement in Saint-Germain, apparently unaware that August is the worst conceivable month to visit. A leaden weariness had settled across the city. I worked on my novel with less enthusiasm than usual, and anyone who could leave the city did so. They were already strolling through the small airy cities of the Côte d'Azur or ambling along the endless beaches of the Atlantic.

Arthur had also already left on his trip, together with Maman and his little friend Giulietta. I remained standing on the train platform and waved at them for a long time, even though I couldn't see anyone on the other side of the mirrored glass.

I felt oddly untethered and abandoned, and didn't know what I should do with myself on this fragmented Thursday.

Then Alexandre called.

'So, did you ditch all the baggage? I'm sure you're dying of boredom, aren't you?'

'How'd you guess?' I replied, concealing the fact that I was really touched. Alexandre was the best. I couldn't wish for a better friend.

'Listen. I'm going to that new jazz club near the Bastille with a few friends. Come along.'

I decided to make an effort. 'Yes, why not,' I said.

Anything was better than hanging out at home with my own gloomy thoughts. Why not jazz? Why not a few drinks? After all, there wasn't anyone I needed to take care of tonight.

We arranged that I would pick up Alexandre at L'espace des rêveurs after the shop closed. And a few hours later, as I walked down the summery, empty Rue de Grenelle, I had no idea that I would find something there that I had already given up searching for.

As I opened the shop door, Alexandre emerged from the back room and held out to me a small, brown leather bag, which dangled from his fingers at the end of narrow straps.

'Look!' he said. 'You were right – it was here after all. Gabrielle thought it was mine, since I have a bag that looks a lot like this one. She stuck it in the closet with some of my other things.'

I gasped – 'You've got to be kidding!' – as I took the small bag that I'd spent the past few weeks delving for.

I had finally given up, accepting that after that fatal Wednesday at Hélène's grave I had left it sitting in some bar. It had seemed like the perfect ending to a black day on which everything that could go wrong had gone wrong, the afternoon after which Sophie had gone missing. The only thing that hadn't been destroyed was all my illusions.

I'd forgotten my agreement with Sophie because after my terrible row with Cathérine, I'd gone straight to Alexandre's shop to unload my anger and disappointment. We had eventually gone to a bar and then to another one. When I drunkenly stumbled into my empty apartment that night (Arthur was spending the night with a friend), my leather satchel and its precious silver disk were suddenly missing.

I had retraced my footsteps the next day – to Alexandre's shop, the bars, wherever we had been. I had even called the Metro Lost and Found Office. I had torn up my apartment in the vain hope that in my inebriated state I had simply dropped the bag somewhere. I searched under my bed and went through the garbage can. However, I eventually gave up. The last message was gone – from whoever in the world had left it. I fantasised about it and became obsessed with the idea that the silver disk would have revealed everything to me. It was the key to me understanding everything. Alexandre had looked at me with pity and said: 'Do you want to know what I think?'

'No!' I shouted, beside myself.

'Nothing's been lost, at least nothing big. It was from Cathérine anyway, whatever might've been on it. Just be glad your wallet wasn't in it – *that* would've been tragic.'

And now the little bag had shown up, out of the blue. I quickly opened it.

'The disk's still in there,' Alexandre remarked nonchalantly. 'I already looked.'

'That makes me feel better. Did you play it?'

'No, of course not.' He grinned. 'I thought we could do that together, right here on my computer. I would enjoy watching Cathérine's confession video. It'll be funny.'

'No way,' I replied, pressing the little bag tighter against my chest.

Whatever was on this disk was meant just for me. I gave Alexandre a determined look, and he relented.

'In that case, I assume you won't be coming to the jazz club, will you?'

I nodded. 'That's right.'

'Then send me a text at least. I'm interested in knowing what's on it. Want to bet it's the pretty neighbour?'

'I don't make bets any more,' I replied.

21

Secret heart

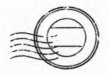

Nobody had never covered the distance between Rue de Grenelle and Rue Jacob in so little time. I practically ran down the narrow street until I reached Boulevard Saint-Germain, where I waited impatiently for a few seconds on the light, before crossing the boulevard against the red. Jogging down Rue Bonaparte, I passed the Deux Magots where tourists sat outside in the evening sun, sipping their glasses of white wine while gazing at the unpretentious old church of Saint-Germain. I rapidly turned right down Rue Jacob, and in just a few steps I was standing in front of my building.

I punched in the combination for the front door, dashed up the three flights of stairs, and shoved my key into the apartment door with trembling hands.

I then switched on my computer, but before I inserted the mystery disk I jumped up and fetched a bottle of wine from the kitchen. I poured myself a large glass. My father had always said: 'With a glass of good red wine, you can handle most things, though perhaps not everything.' I toasted his memory, murmuring: 'I hope you're right, Papa!' before draining half the glass.

Whatever was on that disk, it was going to bring changes.

As single-minded as Orpheus, who received his mysterious message from the radio in the black limousine, I huddled in front of my computer monitor. Who would appear on the screen? Would it really be Cathérine, who had chosen this way to confess her love? Or would Hélène's face materialise on the screen and speak to me – greetings from another world, so to speak? Perhaps my wife had been foresighted enough to record herself before her death and ask someone – Cathérine? – to play the video for me at some point.

I stared mesmerised at the screen, but it remained black.

From the computer's speakers played the first notes of a glockenspiel, followed quickly by the subdued rhythms of a bass guitar. Then a voice that reminded me of Norah Jones started singing a song I'd never heard. The voice of the singer was pleasant and multifaceted, soft, hoarse, dark, childlike.

The song was called 'Secret Heart'. I listened to it again and again, until I understood the full lyrics.

The song focused on the hidden heart of a particular man, and the silky, somewhat brittle voice of the singer asked what his heart was made of, why it was so scared, and if perhaps he was afraid of three simple words, afraid that someone might hear them. Each of the verses ended with a challenge to let his love into his secret heart.

I felt especially moved by one particular part of the song. It addressed the secret that the subject was obviously trying to hide. Ironically, it was the very secret that he so wanted to admit as well.

It was a wonderful song about hidden love, about the fear and pride that you can feel. The song also discussed the benefits of admitting and sharing love.

I tried to find out something about the singer. Her name was Leslie Feist, and she was from Canada, but that didn't help me out.

I wrote out the lyrics and read them line by line as I listened to the song again, its melody now lodged in my head.

The message seemed clear – but was it supposed to reveal something about the feelings of the person who had left the CD for me in the compartment? Or was the song and the challenge it presented meant for me?

Was this about my *secret heart*, my secret feelings that I couldn't show? Or about the secret letters of Montmartre?

And who was the *she* I should let into my heart?

I sat at the desk for hours, drinking one glass of wine after the other and staring at the things I'd found at Hélène's grave over the past few months, which were lined up in a little procession across my desk.

Weren't these all signs of love?

In the middle of the night, I woke up to the sound of the balcony door crashing shut. A summer wind was driving a bevy of white clouds across the moon, floating high and pale above the city. I glanced at the clock: a few minutes after four – the favourite hour of everyone who sleeps poorly. I drank a glass of water and tried to find a different position that would allow me to fall back asleep. I tossed and turned, plumped my pillow, and pulled one leg out from under the covers, but the images kept recurring. People and situations swept through my mind, jumbled up with both spoken and written words. I once again visualised everything I had experienced in recent months – since the day I had begun to write the letters to Hélène. While this was going on, 'Secret Heart' rang in my ears, portraying the images and feelings like a film score.

My heart tightened as I once again saw Hélène in her green dress, on the day we met, her red curls set aflame by the May sun. And then, toward the end, her translucent body, her lovely mouth smiling so pale and brave as her coppery hair gleamed from the white pillow, like a final greeting to me.

But then another face appeared in front of Hélène's, and my heart hammered against the mattress as if wanting to tell me something.

I got up. I got up in the middle of the night and sat at my desk, inspired by an idea. I didn't know if it was good or bad, if it would lead to something or not. However, it was the only thing that seemed to be right to me at this moment.

I pulled out a sheet of stationery and unscrewed my pen, before gazing thoughtfully at the white page for a few minutes.

And then I wrote to Hélène, to the dead wife I adored more than anything, and opened my heart.

My beloved Hélène,

I haven't written for a few weeks now, and there's a reason for that. Your poor husband has found himself in a state of profound confusion. So many exciting things have happened in these past weeks, and I am increasingly doubtful when it comes to my crazy idea that you're the one who's been leaving the signs for me at the grave. I still think that you're watching over me, Hélène, and that your love can transcend death and leave traces in my life. But perhaps those signs aren't necessarily expressed in music boxes, maps or poems by Prévert, but rather in thoughts and feelings.

I've felt like I was going out of my mind these past few months. Like a detective, I have tried to follow the clues, along with Alexandre, and have suspected all sorts of people. And yet over and over again, I came to the conclusion that it was you. It had to be, even if that seemed completely impossible.

I wrote my letters to you, and each response seemed to point to you. However, everything has two sides, which is why I gradually realised that all these signs were leading me back to the cemetery, but also from there back into life.

Before you died, Hélène, you asked that I write to you, about how my life was without you. And now I have fully understood the idea that was behind this request. I mean, the fact that life will go on without you.

I still don't know who is taking my letters and leaving me all the little tokens in the compartment, but that no longer matters so much now. Even if I did have a suspicion, I no longer care if it's you, your friend Cathérine, a lovely stranger, my publisher, or someone else.

What is critical – what truly matters – is that I have opened my heart again – to life, and yes – perhaps also to love.

For a long time, I didn't want to admit this. I tried to run away from it, but I feel something again, Hélène. There is something new, a tender dream that sometimes floats up to the

*surface of my consciousness and feels like a small, trembling bird
in my hand.*

Can it really be true that I've fallen in love again?

*You – who know everything and can see everything from
above – surely know the answer to the question that is keeping
me awake on this night in which sleep is elusive.*

*The truth is: I will always love you, Hélène. And yet someone
else has also found her way into my heart. It is Sophie, the
woman up in the tree whom Arthur discovered on the day I
took my first letter to your grave. The sculptor I occasionally
mentioned to you, but who has tried so hard to guide me back
into the world of the living. She was the one who told me that, in
the end, you need to always choose life over death. She may have
someone else, but that doesn't change the fact that I think about
her and miss her. Her dark eyes, her silvery laugh.*

Do you know what Arthur said to Cathérine?

'Sophie makes Papa laugh again.'

It is astonishing how children can always see the truth.

*And now she has vanished, Hélène! I haven't seen her at the
cemetery in over three weeks, and I don't know what to do about
it. I don't even know where she lives, and she has no idea about
my feelings, which I didn't realise myself for a long time. I will
now entrust them to you, my dear heart.*

*If she would just return to the Cimetière Montmartre, I could
tell her everything. I would take that risk, even if I'm not sure
what will happen in the end.*

*If you fall in love, you have to take your heart in both hands
and risk everything, right?*

I'm writing you this letter in the hope that you will help me, my marvellous angel, who always watches over us. Help me, Hélène!
In love,
Julien

22

The Courtyard of the Conservators

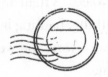

It was very difficult, but I let almost a week go by before returning to the Cimetière Montmartre to see if my night-time letter had found its mysterious recipient.

As I approached Hélène's grave that morning, I at once caught sight of a single red rose glowing amidst the green ivy. My heart skipped a beat. That could mean only one thing – that someone had been to the grave since my previous visit.

I excitedly leaned down to the secret compartment and opened it. My last letter was gone, as well as the opened envelope that had sat there in the cavity untouched for such a long time.

The compartment was empty, completely empty.

I shut it again and looked over at the angel's head. The angel was smiling, and so was I.

My letter seemed to have reached its destination, wherever that happened to be.

For a while, I stood there sunk in thought, hardly daring to believe that over the past six months I had actually written thirty-two letters. There was only one letter to go until I had fulfilled Hélène's last wish and my vow. It was strange, but for the first time, I hoped that Hélène would win her bet.

I strolled through the cemetery, past the old trees, gravestones and statues warming in the sun. They were so familiar to me that I could have found them in the dark.

At the entrance, I heard voices. A man and a woman in work clothes were carrying a stone something, hauling it to a grave where they carefully set it upright. The man swore, the woman laughed. And as she turned around, it was Sophie.

A thousand stones fell away from my heart, and I increased my pace. She was here. She was finally here.

I was so relieved to see her that I didn't think much about what should come next.

'Sophie! Hey, Sophie!' I called and waved.

As she caught sight of me, she flushed darkly.

'Oh, the author,' she said, taking a few tentative steps toward me.

'Where have you been all this time?' I asked.

The man in a dark grey work apron glanced over at us and studied me intently. He was older, and had a small moustache and alert brown eyes.

'Papa, this is Julien Azoulay,' Sophie declared in lieu of an answer, and the old man shook my hand so hard I almost fell to my knees. His handshake was just as firm as his daughter's. 'He's an author.'

He didn't look particularly impressed.

'And this is my father, Gustave Claudel.'

Gustave – hadn't I heard that name somewhere?

'We were just bringing a statue over from the workshop. It's as good as new again. The head and arms, everything had to be repaired ...' Sophie was talking a blue streak. Her cheeks were pink, and she kept shooting me odd glances.

The old man put his hands on his hips and straightened his lower back. 'This thing weighs a ton – we should've asked Philippe for help like I said. You shouldn't be carrying anything so heavy, *ma petite.*'

Confused, I looked from one to the other.

Shouldn't carry anything so heavy? Why not?

'But ... What happened?' I asked. 'Where were you the past few weeks?'

'Ah ... I sprained my ankle,' Sophie admitted ruefully.

'She fell out of a tree, silly girl.' Gustave Claudel shook his head. 'Why does she always have to scamper around on top of things like a little monkey? On walls, in trees. I've told her that a million times. Someday she's going to break her neck.'

Sophie watched me, a mixture of defiance and unease written across her face. Hadn't I told her the same thing? On that day when she had teetered up on the wall and called out to me that I was in a bad mood. On that awful Wednesday when I hadn't come back to pick her up because I'd been sitting on the grave wall with Cathérine, totally done in. I suddenly remembered the little sound that had come from the old chestnut tree. Hadn't it sounded like a sneeze? Had Sophie possibly heard everything? My accusations, my furious shouting – I'd been loud enough. My assertion that she was just a random acquaintance and that I didn't think I could ever fall in love again?

I stared at her and silently begged her forgiveness.

Sophie didn't move. She just stood there in her cap, her lips pressed into a hard line.

Gustave scratched the back of his head. He seemed to sense the churning vibes at play between his daughter and me. He probably thought I was a very strange young man. An author to boot. Writers were bound to be questionable in the old stone worker's eyes. He gave a curt nod to bring the matter to an end.

'My pleasure, Monsieur,' he said, turning his back on me and taking a few steps toward the grave. 'Come on, Sophie. We have to get this thing back in place.'

'No, wait!' I begged quietly.

She stopped and threw me a mocking look.

'Not a good time, author.'

'I don't care. I . . . I would like to tell you something, Sophie, but I don't trust myself to.'

'Oh! That again! The *secret*?' She raised her eyebrows.

'No. This time it's something else. Something that has to do with you and me. With *us*!' I whispered nervously, suggestively. I placed my hand over my heart.

Her eyes widened, and she bit her lower lip as she gazed at me thoughtfully.

'I would also like to tell you something, Julien,' she said hesitantly. 'But I trust myself even less than you do.'

'Are you coming, Sophie?'

'I'm coming, *Chouchou*,' she called, shooting me an apologetic look. 'I have to go, or Papa will get impatient. Can you come back this afternoon, Julien? Around four or so?'

I nodded, and my heart leaped into my throat.

Sophie watched me, and my world was reflected in the darkness of her eyes.

'Then we'll tell each other everything,' she whispered before she turned around and ran to her father.

To *Chouchou*.

I tried to somehow kill the next few hours. I prowled around Montmartre, working my way up and down the alleys. I eventually sat down in the little park located at the foot of the Sacré-Cœur. Every few minutes I saw the *funiculaire* climb up the hill, the small silvery car that ferries its passengers from the bottom of Montmartre up to the white basilica. After a while, the park grew too crowded and loud, so I stood up and walked over to the other side of the hill, where I turned down a side street close to the Musée Montmartre and found a quiet café. I ordered something to drink and forced myself to eat a sandwich as I smoked a cigarette. I sat there and waited, but I didn't mind. I gazed up into the cloudless summer sky and yearned for the afternoon to end, like someone who longs for morning after a night spent with a toothache. Only in my case, I wasn't plagued by the painful throbbing of a tooth, but by the anxious thumping of my heart, which simply refused to settle down.

Sophie was back. She was unattached. And *Chouchou* was her father! I had almost hugged the old man when I realised this.

And under these circumstances, was it really so presumptuous of me to think that Sophie's friendliness had been motivated by more than compassion? That she might actually feel something for me – for me, this egocentric, morose, blind Orpheus? This man who had stared at nothing except a closed door? This man who was now ready to offer her his heart – even if she was sitting on the highest wall in all of Paris?

Yes, we will tell each other everything, I thought, as I stirred my espresso and smiled contentedly. I kept thinking this as I strode in joyful anticipation down the street that led to the Cimetière Montmartre. I kept thinking this as I stepped through the gate, my heart pounding, expecting to hear Sophie call my name at any moment.

But the cemetery was silent. The sun continued to arc through the sky, and the sculptor was nowhere to be seen.

I nervously fingered a cigarette out of my packet, and walked up and down the paths as I puffed on it. It was four o'clock, and we had definitely fixed to meet. Where was she? I took an uneasy seat on a bench close to the gate and watched for her.

It was four-thirty, then five, and still no sign of Sophie. I finally jumped back up and decided to go to Hélène's grave and wait there. Maybe Sophie would come here.

I looked all around, and everything seemed peaceful and unchanged. The angel still smiled its enigmatic smile, and a bird fluttered in the old chestnut tree. However, the red rose was no longer sitting in the green ivy. Someone had placed it on top of the marble gravestone.

Someone?

I knelt down and opened the compartment.

I saw the small white envelope right away.

It was so light, as if it contained nothing except air. But when I tore it open, a small card fell out of it:

Sophie Claudel
La Cour des Conservateurs
Rue d'Orchampt
Paris

I swayed there for a moment, and the letters swam before my eyes. Sophie wasn't here, but her calling card was sitting in the secret compartment. And now everything made sense. Sophie's embarrassment. Her hesitation. What she trusted herself so little to reveal to me.

The heart of stone, the brochure from the Musée Rodin where I had admired the sculptures by Camille Claudel without understanding why I was there. The tickets for *Orphée*, the theatre on Montmartre where she had 'coincidentally' shown up and let me discover her. The wall to which the map had led me as a way to tell me 'I love you!' The CD with the song 'Secret Heart'. It had all been Sophie.

She had read my letters.

She had provided the answers.

The blood rushed to my head as I hurried out of the cemetery. I knew the little street, which was located behind the shadowy Place Émile Goudeau. My heart raced as I climbed up the road.

My eyes searched each building I passed along Rue d'Orchampt, until I caught sight of the enamel sign with a blue border. It bore the words La Cour des Conservateurs in sweeping script – The Courtyard of the Conservators.

I pushed open the gate and entered a cobblestone courtyard, whose right-hand side housed a workshop for wood conservators. On the left side was the stone workers' atelier. The door was standing open, and I stepped inside.

It smelled of dust and paint, and my gaze swept across this magical garden peopled with stone figures with upraised arms, some draped in pale cloths. My eyes took in the white marble hands, heads and feet strewn across a large table, and then travelled on to the elaborate sculptures that stretched up to the ceiling. I saw the long workbench that was standing underneath the large window on the opposite wall, before moving on to the saws, chisels and mallets that were lined up along it like tin soldiers.

'Hello?' I called. 'Is anyone here?'

After a clatter, the door to the back room opened with a quiet squeak. Gustave Claudel stood there in his grey work apron, his eyes warm and amiable.

'She's up in her apartment,' he declared, pointing to the building at the back of the courtyard. 'She's expecting you.'

23

I had so hoped it was you

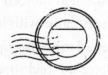

Sophie's apartment was located on the fourth floor. I ran up the well-worn wooden steps, but before I could press the doorbell, the door was opened from the inside.

Breathless and pale, Sophie stood before me. She was wearing a soft lilac dress, and her eyes were huge in the dim light of the hallway.

For a few seconds, we just mutely looked at each other, our eyes exploring the faces we dared not touch yet. She then twirled around toward a small wooden chest on a table, only to turn back around to hold out a bundle of letters to me.

'Can you forgive me?' she asked quietly, her eyes shining.

I shook my head and gently took the letters from her.

'No, I'm the one who needs your forgiveness!' I said. 'I was such an idiot.'

I cupped her face in her hands. All that existed at this moment were her and me. As our lips met over and over again, unable to stop, we whispered our love to each other. And the letters floated, as lightly as leaves, to the floor.

I didn't return to Rue Jacob that night. I stayed on Montmartre, in a tiny, crooked attic apartment where I suddenly and unexpectedly discovered happiness.

Sophie and I told each other everything that evening.

She told me about how she had noticed me in the cemetery – the miserable man who sometimes came with his small son. How one day after we had met, she happened to see me open the gravestone and put something inside it. How later she had slipped over to Hélène's grave and discovered the secret compartment.

'And then I found all the letters. I can't tell you how moved I was by them. Touched, and a little shocked, as well. I picked up the top letter – I couldn't help it. I read it, Julien, but not out of nosiness.' She looked at me affectionately. 'I fell in love with you – the first day we met, when you were searching for Arthur and I was sitting up on the wall. Remember that?'

'Oh, Sophie, how could I forget!' I kissed her tenderly, as she leaned back against me. 'It was so magical. Good grief, I thought you were a creature from another world when I saw Arthur standing there, talking to the tree. I was so happy to find him again, and then it was you sitting up there. And afterward, we went to L'Artiste. I think that was the first truly enjoyable evening since Hélène's death, but I was still so eaten up by my own misery . . .'

She nodded. 'I know, Julien. When I read that letter, it felt like my heart turned inside out. You were so distraught. You begged Hélène for a sign, and I . . .'

She broke off for a moment, as tears welled in her eyes.

'I was so sad for you, Julien, and I wanted to help you somehow.' She leaned back into the sofa where we were sitting next to each other. 'And so, I read all your letters, from the first through the latest one you had brought to the grave. I was shocked. I knew you weren't doing well and how much you missed your wife, but that . . .'

She shook her head. 'I just wanted to do something to help you feel happy again. I wanted to help distract your thoughts. And then I had the idea about the answers.' She smiled. 'I left a trail for you and hoped that eventually it would lead you to me. To be honest, I was a little surprised you didn't think of me much earlier . . .'

'But I *did* think of you, Sophie,' I cut in. 'Right at the start, I went through all the possible solutions. But you had a boyfriend who was always calling you. How could I know that *Chouchou* was your father? Why do you call him that anyway?'

She grinned. 'It dates back to my nursery-school days. My mother had always called Papa *mon petit chou*, and I turned that into *chouchou* at some point.'

'The last great secret.' I brushed a strand of hair from her forehead. 'No, the next to last. Why did the thing with the letters stop so abruptly?' I looked at her searchingly, and she turned red. 'Were your feelings hurt when I forgot our date?'

'Well, yes,' she whispered. 'What can I say? You were at the grave for so long. You didn't came back, so I followed you. I saw Cathérine standing at the grave with the letter, and you yelling angrily at her. I quickly climbed up the old chestnut tree to hide.'

'And you heard everything from up in your hiding place?'

She nodded. 'You were so upset about the letters, and you just kept yelling that it was private, *private*! And in one horrible, scary moment, I realised what I had actually done. If you could hammer a good friend into the ground like that, how would you react when you found out that I was the one who had opened your letters and read them?'

She looked at me.

'My lovely house of cards collapsed in one fell swoop, everything I thought I was building for us. And then you went on to say that I was just a random person you'd met at the cemetery.'

'Yes.' I nodded unhappily. 'I'm so sorry, Sophie. I regretted that the moment I said it. I was just so annoyed at Cathérine for never stopping with all her questions.' I picked up her hand. 'You were never just a random person to me, Sophie,' I said quietly.

'I know that. Now. But when I heard you say that, it was a huge shock for me.'

'And you fell out of the tree because of that?'

'No, no.' She smiled. 'You'd have heard if I'd tumbled out of the tree like some windfall apple. After you stormed off, I stayed up on my branch for a while longer, feeling quite awful. When I finally decided to climb down, I slipped, and when I hit the ground I sprained my ankle. It hurt so badly I thought I'd broken it. And this was right after you'd insisted that you'd never fall in love again.' She placed her hand on her heart and grimaced drolly. 'I sobbed all the way down the path.'

'Oh no . . .' I could imagine her hobbling down the cemetery path. 'It was a really bad day for both of us. And then?'

'I didn't go back to the cemetery for several weeks. I could hardly walk, much less work. I had plenty of time to think about everything, which seemed more and more hopeless. Until ...'

'Until you saw my last letter to Hélène.'

'Yes.' She nodded, her face brightening. 'I was ecstatic when I read that you missed me. That in the end, you'd actually fallen in love – with me!'

She wrinkled her forehead. 'But then I remembered that you still didn't know who had taken all the letters, and I was suddenly scared that you'd never forgive me ...' She plucked at her dress, embarrassed. 'Are you really not angry with me, Julien? You must know one thing: I only did it out of love. I love you, Julien.'

She turned toward me, and I couldn't help thinking about the first time I had seen this face, that day when she had sat above me and gazed down from her wall, the day I had thought for a heartbeat that she was a pixie. And then my thoughts turned to our night-time stroll through silent Montmartre, that magical hour before our ways parted and I'd watched with a pang of regret as she walked away. That was the moment of my first inkling, my first thought, my first wish, which at the time, I didn't dare follow through to its full extent.

I pulled her fiercely into my arms.

'Oh, Sophie,' I whispered, burying my face in her hair. 'I had so hoped it was you.'

As she later lay sleeping in my arms, I stared for a long time into the night's darkness, which wasn't as dark as usual due to a single silver beam that fell through the opened window. I thought how life is both sad and humorous, horrifying in its injustice yet full of wonder at the same time.

And unbelievably beautiful.

Epilogue

Montmartre – that famous hill on the northern edge of Paris, where tourists cluster around the street painters on the Place du Tertre as they create artworks of dubious quality, where in late summer couples ramble through the lively streets hand in hand before sinking down a little breathless on the steps of the Sacré-Cœur, to gaze in amazement across the city shimmering in the final gentle rosy glow before nightfall – Montmartre is home to a cemetery. It is a very old cemetery, complete with dirt paths and long shady drives that meander under lindens and maples. It even uses names and numbers, which make it seem like a real town. A very silent town. Some of the people resting here are famous. You can find graves ornamented with artistic monuments and angelic figures in sweeping stone garments, their arms gracefully outstretched, their eyes fixed on the sky.

A dark-haired man enters the cemetery, carrying a giant bouquet of roses. He stops at a grave known only to a few people. No one famous slumbers here. No author, musician or painter. This isn't the Lady of the Camellias, either. Just someone who had been deeply loved.

Nonetheless, the angel on the bronze tablet affixed to the marble gravestone is one of the loveliest here. The woman's face – earnest, perhaps even serene – gazes out with a hint of a smile, her long hair billowing around her face as if being tossed by a wind at her back.

The man pauses, listening to the laughter of a child who is waiting outside the cemetery gate with a young woman.

It is a later summer day. A butterfly flutters through the air, finally landing on the gravestone where it beats its wings a few times.

The man pulls a letter out of his pocket, the last of thirty-three letters he has written to his wife. He places it in the secret compartment in the gravestone and shuts the little door. He then takes a step back and glances one last time at the bronze angel with its familiar feathers, and lays the bouquet of roses on the grave – certainly the largest to be found anywhere in the entire Cimetière Montmartre.

'You were so smart, Hélène,' he says, his smile a little askew. 'It's obvious you somehow managed to orchestrate everything to win your bet. I know you, Hélène, you simply can't lose. Never could.'

The man lingers a moment longer. He studies the peaceful face of the lovely angel, and for a millisecond he thinks he sees the corner of its mouth twitch upward.

'Au revoir, Hélène,' he says before turning and walking back down the path with a smile on his face.

He had been unprepared for what had happened, just as unprepared as anyone could be for the arrival of happiness or love. And yet, both of them are always there. He knows that now.

His small son and the woman he loves are waiting for him at the cemetery gate. They take each other's hands and stroll out into the sunlit day.

The man's name is Julien Azoulay.

And I happen to be Julien Azoulay.

Dearest Hélène,

This is the last of my letters to you. I have written you thirty-three letters, just as I promised. When you forced this oath out of me, Hélène, I was so emotionally broken that I never would have believed what you told me: that by the time I reached this last letter, my life would take a turn for the better. I hated it when you said that. I didn't want to hear it, and I fought against it tooth and nail.

And yet, wonder of wonders, that is exactly what has happened, Hélène.

I have actually fallen in love. It's more than that – I love, and I am loved. Every morning, I am astonished anew by this incredible blessing.

A year ago, I was the unhappiest man in the world. My heart had turned to stone, was surrounded by a wall. And then this woman entered my life. She is so very different from you, Hélène, and yet, I love her with all my heart. Can you believe that?

I cannot remember who once said: 'The heart is a very, very resilient little muscle.'

But you know what, Hélène? I'm so glad it is.

And even if you weren't the one who left all those little things for me in the secret compartment, I still believe in miracles. I sometimes think that it was you who sent that butterfly that one day, the one that Arthur chased and that led us to Sophie. And who knows? Maybe that really is what happened.

Arthur immediately accepted Sophie into his heart. It took me a little longer, but then again I'm just a dumb man, as Sophie sometimes teases.

I didn't go to Honfleur this summer.

I wanted to stay with Sophie, whom I had just found.

At first, Maman was disappointed when I called to tell her that I wouldn't be joining them at the coast. However, when I explained that I was sitting next to the girl she had been hoping was walking around somewhere, who could love her Julien, she was simply happy for me.

'Oh, my child,' she repeated huskily. 'Oh, my child!'

You always remain a child to your mother, even if you are eighty years old. I might smile at this, but sometimes I worry a little about the day there will no longer be anyone to say that to me. Oh, my child!

The summer is almost over now. The summer break has ended, and people are returning to Paris.

Camille had her baby a few days ago – an adorable girl – Pauline. We were all there for it. Aunt Carole was over the moon, and even old Paul had a lucid moment when she placed the baby in his arms. He said it was the most precious treasure, such a small creature.

The rest of us stood there, deeply moved, and Arthur was perfectly still when the baby reached for his finger and wrapped her tiny fingers around it.

Arthur is still 'going' with Giulietta. She came over again the other day, and I heard him say to her that he was so happy that his Papa had someone to go with again.

Sophie still has her attic apartment in the restorers' courtyard, but she comes over almost every day after work and stays the night. It is wonderful to have a woman in the apartment again who can fill my life with light. No, not just any woman, but Sophie alone. Unlike Alexandre, I don't believe that you can fall in love with just anyone. When Alexandre heard that Sophie was the one behind it all, he claimed that he'd known all along. Typical! He'd been the one betting that it was your friend. I'm very glad that Cathérine has apparently got through her crisis. She greeted Sophie, Arthur and me very amicably in the entry area when we ran into her recently. She was in the company of a friendly man she introduced as her new co-worker.

And someone else is happy, too. He interrupted me when I was writing my first letter to you, Hélène, and he ended up interrupting me as I wrote this last one. I had just sat down at my desk when Jean-Pierre Favre called to see how the novel was going.

'The novel's coming along great,' I told him truthfully. 'I'm almost done with it. However . . . ' I hesitated.

'However?' he asked impatiently. 'Stop leaving me in such suspense, Azoulay!'

'However, it's turned into a very different book.'

'Okay?'

'What would you think of a love story that starts out in a cemetery?'

'In a cemetery,' he repeated, considering this for a moment. 'Hmm. Well, why not? In a cemetery, that sounds original . . . I like it! All good novels start with a funeral. But . . . does the story have a happy ending?'

'Of course,' I said. 'After all, I write romantic comedies.'

He laughed.

'Very good, Azoulay, very good. But the book about the publisher who dances around in the moonlight, let's not shelve it completely, après tout?'

'Definitely not,' I replied. 'That'll be the next one I write.'

'Wonderful! I can tell that you've found your old joie de vivre, Azoulay,' Jean-Pierre Favre declared happily.

And he's right, my old publisher. My life was so heavy, and now it has grown light again. Perhaps not as light as air, but still very light. I'm happy, Hélène. I never would have thought I'd say that again. I'm so filled with my love for Sophie, but I often think lovingly about you. I believe my heart is large enough for both of you. But my place is here, Hélène, and yours is in the cemetery, or somewhere between the stars.

This is my final letter to you, my angel, and I don't think that anyone will read it except for you. It will sit in your gravestone until perhaps, many years from now, someone will find it there and be amazed at this token of a great love.

I may be long dead by then, and we will have each other again, like once in May. But until then, I will live and love.

Yours,

Julien

Postface

This novel is a work of fiction, and yet it is filled with things and incidents that actually did or possibly could occur.

The idea for this novel came to me several years ago when I was walking around an old cemetery one spring. It was not the Cimetière Montmartre, which I chose for this book because I find it so unique. It was a small enchanting graveyard far from Paris.

In this small cemetery, there is an angel that served as the model for the bronze angel on Hélène's grave. This was also where I found that verse about the lovers in May, which touched me so deeply that it inspired me to write this story.

You could say that I stumbled across it, so to speak, because the three lines were inscribed in a round slab that was set into one of the pathways. The letters had been buried under such a thick layer of gravel that I had to carefully brush the stones away before I could make out the words.

I have thought a lot about these unknown lovers, and hope with all my heart that they are now together again, like once in May.

It has been a long time since anyone was buried in this small cemetery with its old trees, green bushes and rolling meadows. These days, old men sit here in the sunshine and read newspapers on the green wooden benches. In the summer, young students spread their beach towels on the grass under the trees and read their books. Couples stroll leisurely down the paths, friends tell each other their secrets, young parents push their strollers on walks. Sometimes, pearly lanterns are strung between the graves, which is particularly captivating, and you can hear the bright laughter of children having birthday picnics here with their mothers.

I love the idea that in this peaceful place, where many years ago the dead found their final resting places, life goes on. This is the very same ground on which small feet trample, people dwell on their thoughts, and others exchange smiles.

I think the dead take delight in this. I believe that they watch over us, the living, kindly and indulgently; that we know so very little about what is possible in the realm between heaven and earth; and that they always want to remind us that love is the answer to all our questions.

Paris, May 2018

Nicolas Barreau is both the name of an acclaimed Parisian writer of mixed parentage, who studied at the Sorbonne and worked in a bookshop on the Rive Gauche . . . and a pseudonym concealing the identity of a mysterious literary figure, unreachable except through his editor.